ONCE UPON A TIME:

A Collection of African Folk-tales & Proverbs

UKACHUKWU OKORIE

FIRST PUBLISHED BY SKYLINE PUBLISHSHING
(Rep. of Ireland 2016)
(T/A NEW AGE PUBLISHERS)
www.skylinebureau.com/publishing

British Library Cataloguing in Publication Data
A catalogue record for this book is available from the
British Library

ISBN : 978-0-9576498-9-7

Printed in the United Kingdom, 2016.

Table of Contents

SECTION ONE FOLKTALES

SECTION TWO

SECTION THREE : Proverbs (Bonus Section)

Dedication

This book is dedicated to UNICEF, "whose works and influences are helping to overcome the obstacles that poverty, violence, disease and discrimination place in a child's path." In our world today, children continue to die in horrendous situations and this should not be so. Development should be centered on empowering these young ones because they are the future. It is with this thought in mind that I dedicate this book to all children, and those working to make the world a better and safer place for Mankind.

Acknowledgment

Kudos to Milada Bacik for drawing the illustrations. I wish to thank my friend Lylyan Fotabong and Aidan Lucid for their assistance with the manuscript. My special acknowledgment goes to my late grandfather Thompson Nnanna Okorie (Uyokanjo), his descendants born and unborn. Special thanks to Evangeline Ngozi Omini for her motherly love. As usual, I appreciate my siblings, particularly Ijeoma Oluhara Iroegbu who has become a beacon of truth and support for me. To my critics, colleagues, friends, well wishers and fans too numerous to mention, you are acknowledged. Special love to you AfricaWorld News family for your hard work in spreading us around the world.

Introduction

Before the introduction of the European Classroom System of Education in some parts of Africa, the moonlight provided many uses such as time to play games and time for kindred-style gatherings. In these gatherings, elders told many tales and wise sayings and children learnt wisdom from them. This tradition of moonlight games and storytelling has continued to evolve in most parts of Africa, even in the 21st century.

It is the evolution of moonlight storytelling that has made me want to tell you some of these tales. Some of them are hundreds of years old, while others were narrated to me by my grandfather. My grandfather worked for colonial authorities and when he retired from the service, he became a Great Counsellor. With both careers, he socialised with diverse groups of people and soon was noted as a "bridge" between the old Africa and the new one. He was well known for his integrity and also as a great storyteller. He told us - his grandchildren - stories that shaped his world and divulged great tales that came in many forms such as, folktales, fairy-tales, eyewitness accounts and stories of family traditions.

Back in those days, it was customary for us to leave our home in the city to spend Christmas at our countryside home where our grandfather also lived. During one of our visits, in the cold Harmattan breeze when the moon was at its fullest, we gathered at the feet of our grandfather for him to tell us stories. He chewed a kola nut to begin the first story of the night and one of my cousins asked him,

"Grandpa, why do you always eat the kola nut before beginning your stories?"

"Child, it is the tradition of my ancestors, which is why I do it in your presence. The chameleon says that he will never abandon the dignified walking ways of his fathers just because the bush is burning," he answered.

So, too, I will not abandon the tradition of my people just because times are changing.

With this, I begin a journey into what used to be and still is the core of moonlight gatherings in many parts of Africa.

Section One

Fairy-Tales

1

How the Dog Became a Domestic Animal

My grandfather asked, "Children, can any of you tell me why dogs live with human beings?"

"No," we replied and he started to tell us this tale.

Once upon a time in the Animal Kingdom where humans lived peacefully side by side with other animals, there was a great famine. The famine was caused by an attack on crops by the Locust's family when one of their friends was assaulted by a group of other animals in the jungle. In retaliation, they ate all green leaves and left the rest to dry. This was to serve as a warning to other animals for the injustice meted out to their friend. In response, the Animal Council banished the Locusts from the kingdom but their expulsion did not resolve the food scarcity. Rather, the dearth continued to ravage the tranquillity that existed in the kingdom and starvation became rife.

The food shortages caused pandemonium among all animals and each of them devised means to tackle the impending starvation. Humans who formed the biggest animal group were the first to run out of food supplies. They failed to heed to warnings and lavished the last of their stock in merriment. They were soon left with nothing and began begging for food from one animal to the other. The other animals gave them their last food crumbs for fear that humans could besiege terror on them, especially as they believed in the saying "a hungry man is an angry man".

Not long after this, most animals also ran out of stock and very little food was left in the kingdom. As starvation settled in, humans resorted to extreme measures and began to poach from other animals' barns. One night, an animal caught a human stealing from his barn of yams. The human feared that the animal would report him and so the human strangled the animal. The man then ate the animal so as to get rid of all traces of evidence of the killing. This soon became a way of life for humans to kill other animals and use them as food if they were caught pilfering.

Meanwhile, the disappearances of animals stirred further problems and instilled fear in all dwellers of the kingdom. This made the dog carry out an independent investigation without informing other animals. His hope was to resolve the cold cases and surprise other animals with his ingenuity. During one of his investigative trips, he caught a human strangling an antelope but was too frightened by the strength demonstrated by the human that he was unable to intervene to rescue the antelope or attack the human.

The man stood face to face with the dog, realising that he had been caught again. He went for the dog but terrified by the strength displayed by the human, the animal hurriedly assured the man that he was never going to tell anyone of his finding. He asked the man to spare his life and in return he would never disclose what he had witnessed. When the human heard his plea, he asked the dog to take a vow of "Trust and perpetual friendship" whereby the dog agreed to never reveal what he had witnessed. The human, on the other hand, vowed that he would never prey on dogs.

Back at home in the kingdom, the famine became ferocious and more and more animals vanished. The Leopard too became desperate to get answers on why animals were vanishing and set up his own independent investigation. While out on an investigative trip, he came upon a young human who was roasting the remains of a Grass Cutter by the side of a bush stream. The sheer shock and horror of what he saw incensed him to get revenge on the perpetrator and he chased after the young man, biting off the human's windpipe.

This discovery by the Leopard, caused mayhem in the animal kingdom and forced the Animal Council to establish a

Jungle Court. The court then set up an inquest to unravel the barbaric acts that were being committed. The court warned that while the inquest was going on, anyone involved or caught in these acts will be burnt to ashes, alongside their offspring.

As the jungle inquest went on, the humans began packing their belongings in the silence of the night, for fear of what would happen to them if the inquest found them guilty. They moved to an undisclosed destination to build homes and start a new life. On the final trip to move the last of their belongings out of the animal kingdom, the dog and his family, fearing that the wrath of other animals would turn on them if they were caught in aiding and abetting humans, followed the humans into their new land.The rest of the animals woke up one morning to the discovery that the humans and dogs were gone. The court passed a resolution that from that moment onwards, humans and dogs were their enemies because they had unjustly sent souls to the great beyond.

In addition to this declaration, the Leopard was assigned to execute the Jungle Judgement that was to kill humans whenever they ventured into their former home.

As they settled in their new abode in another jungle, the dog became humans' best friend, so much so that they decided to live together. From time to time, they all go back together to their former home to continue from where the humans stopped hunting other animals.

"And that, children, is my story tonight," my grandfather ended.

2

The Proud Woodpecker

Once upon a time in the realm of heavenly birds, there was constant struggle, challenge and competition to become the best of all birds. It was also "en vogue" for birds to belong to the upper class. In this kingdom there also lived the Woodpecker. It is a very proud bird that lives an upper class lifestyle, and tells lies and boasts to its "buddies".

The struggle to become a member of the upper class was so fierce that the Woodpecker resorted to fraudulent means to meet and maintain his standards. One of his deceitful survival tactics was to brag that he possessed better talents than others. One day while sitting with other birds, the Woodpecker boasted about one of his potentials. He said that he would chop down the trunk of an Iroko Tree with just his beak, as a mark of respect if and when his mother died.

Suddenly, the Woodpecker became ill from a painful ulcer beneath his beak. For many days, he was unable to talk or even eat, let alone chop the trunk of a tree with his

13

beak. Around this time, his mother died and the other birds, which he had sworn to, challenged him to keep his oath. But the Woodpecker, who could neither talk nor eat, was unable to chop the trunk of the Iroko Tree with his beak as he had proudly claimed.

3

Why the Rat and Cat Are Enemies

Once upon a time the Cat and Rat lived together in unity with their Master who was human. They all grew up loving one another. They not only shared the same bed but they also ate from the same pots and plates. The Master, however, loved the Rat more than the Cat because of its size and cunningness and went as far as willing his entire property to the Rat in the case of his death.

This act of generosity was nonetheless not enough for the Rat. He wanted the properties sooner rather than later. So, he poisoned his master in order to enrich himself with his master's possessions and belong to the crème de la crème of society. After his master died, he accused the Cat of the atrocious act. This infuriated the Cat who loved his master and was still mourning the human's demise. The Cat brought the allegation to the other animals and appealed for a search of the murderer. The other animals agreed with him deciding that both Mr Cat and Mr Rat would take an oath to determine the culprit.

At the beginning, the Rat supported this decision to prove his innocence but then began to change his tactics. He heard that the repercussion for failing the oath was death; consequently he would die if he took the oath. The prospect of death terrified him and he decided to escape from the house on the day of the oath ceremony. He believed that staying away from the oath would allow him to return at a later stage to continue with his plan.

His plan, however, backfired when the animals ruled that he was guilty of killing their master. As a result, they willed the entire property of the Master to the Cat and left the Rat with nothing. The ruling vindicated the Cat but did not satisfy him. He told the animals that although he was happy with their generosity, he felt that it was not enough to undo the evil act that the Rat had committed. He then resolved that he would never share anything again with the Rat and would avenge the death of his master.

The Rat was left alone and went into hiding for fear of what would happen to him if he was seen and caught. After spending a long time alone, he felt very depressed and returned to the family home for reconciliation, but the Cat had made up his mind that he would never forgive him. From time to time, the Rat sneaked in intermittently but the Cat gave chase and wanted to kill the Rat for the crime he committed.

From then onwards, the Cat and Rat became enemies.

4

Hippopotamus and The River Birds

Many years ago in a remote village, it was custom for elders to organise storytelling nights for children. At that time, the tradition required that elders told stories to kids and teenagers on the night of every Eight Market Day, especially during the season of the Moon. It was also conventional that the eldest man in the family would, from time to time, delegate another elder to tell stories, folktales and legendary tales, and also educate the children on certain aspects of the culture. The children were allowed to ask questions and some questions prompted the elders to tell stories that had traditional lessons, taboos and ethical undertones.

On one of these nights, one of the children asked to know the full story of the hippopotamus and the river birds. The elder responded by telling them the following story.

*   *   *

Once upon a time in the land of animals, there was an epidemic that spread like wildfire. The epidemic was caused by carnivorous animals that ate flesh and abandoned the rest to decay. Worms then fed on the decayed flesh to develop their life circle and this system of reproduction caused the virus to spread further and faster. The epidemic soon threatened all animals, especially the bigger ones that ate flesh.

The Animal Medical Council met urgently and came out with a solution called "Operation Cleaning Exercise" in an attempt to stop the virus from making animals extinct. The operation involved smaller animals going through the mouths of bigger animals and picking up the worms and decayed particles. The ideology was to prevent the virus from ravaging the inner chambers of the bigger animals' body systems.

The ruling did not please smaller animals such as the Squirrel and Grass Cutter who felt that they were forced to risk their lives to save others. Unfortunately, it was a decree and they had to oblige to it. So they decided to use the opportunity to retaliate on bigger animals such as Cats, Lions, Tigers and Wolves who continually bullied them, and had devoured some of their kin during the Great Famine.

The plan by the smaller animals, however, failed when the first group that started the operation was caught, killed and eaten by the big animals. The Animal Medical Council sat for a second time and appealed to the bigger animals to stop killing the smaller ones but this again was futile.

In response, the rest of the smaller animals formulated a second plan and it was to spread more of the virus. They agreed to continue with Operation Cleaning Exercise, but this time they were pushing the worms further into the throats of the bigger animals and coming out of their mouths as fast as they could, before the bigger animals moved their jaws to grind them.

As the epidemic raged on and some of the bigger animals continued to devour the smaller animals, the Hippopotamus was one of the few bigger animals that did not prey on the smaller ones. As an alternative, the "Big One", as it was fondly called, consulted the Birds on the River Banks for a solution to the pandemic.

The River Birds sent a few of their kin as sacrificial lambs to continue with Operation Cleaning Exercise. The new partnership between the River Birds and the Hippopotamus was successful and most of the latter survived the epidemic. This act of benevolence shown by the River Birds created an unprecedented bond with the Hippopotamus. It also describes why the Hippopotamus is hardly seen without the River Birds - still known to be sticking around to fight off worms and ants that threaten their big friend.

*   *   *

The story also explains a widely used adage by African elders, which is, "It is not love, but the quest for cleanliness that makes the Hippopotamus open its mouth wide for the River Bird to peck at."

5

The Tortoise and The Heavenly Feast

The art of storytelling is classified under the oral source of history and has existed for many thousands of years. It could even be said to be as old as man. In addition, scientists and archaeologists have put storytelling at the cradle of man's development, and as in other civilisations, storytelling has been at the centre of cultural transformation of Africa. Thus it would not be an overstatement if I affirmed that as civilisation started in Africa, so too was the art of storytelling

Before the introduction of Western form of Education in Africa, Africans kept records of their past and experiences in oral documentation. Some of the oral sources included genealogical stories, fairytales and proverbial illustrations. These oral archives have continued to be an important avenue for recollection, reflection and reconstruction of issues in African societies. Also, generations upon generations carry on relaying the past to the present day generation so as to continue to preserve the African culture. As a result, oral lessons continue to be organised for children and they are taught vicissitudes, short comings and general knowledge. While these classes are important in a typical African society, fairytales have, however, won the appeal of the young minds.

When I was 10 years old, I travelled with my parents to our country home for Christmas celebrations, as was the routine in my part of Africa. I loved this routine but nothing made me happier than joining my young relatives to gather round our storytellers for storytelling nights. On one of the nights, when the moon was at its fullest and the atmosphere was seduced by the Harmattan wind, we gathered round the feet of our grandfather,

"My children, I have a very interesting story to tell you all tonight," he said and then cleared his throat.

"Tell us so that we may be happy," we responded.

*   *   *

Once upon a time in the land of the forests where every creature, except humans, lived, the Creator was the ruler. He organised a big feast in the heavens and invited all birds of the forest. He left out other animals because they had no wings that could enable them to fly or travel far in the sky like the birds. Also, the Creator considered that other animals were bullies and that they continued to intimidate the birds, which was wrong. When the birds received the invitation, they were overjoyed by the privilege and hoped that they would have great fun and merriment with their Chief Host, the Creator.

In addition to the animals in this kingdom, was the Tortoise. He was one of the smallest animals and was loved and respected by all others. He was considered to be realistic and diplomatic in approach and in managing crises. The birds also loved him because they felt that his judgement on matters that affected them was always sensible. Therefore, they invited him to the feast in order to reciprocate his kindness towards them. The Tortoise, however, had no wings and hence could not fly to the venue. This created a problem among the birds who did not want to let the Tortoise down.

The birds held an emergency meeting and agreed that they would each lend the Tortoise wings so that he could be able to fly with them. In one of the preparatory meetings before taking to the sky, the Tortoise proposed that each of the invitees should choose a special name, which will serve as their reference in Heaven. Unaware of his trickery, the birds all chose the names they would like to be called and the Tortoise chose the name, "All of You".

On the day of the feast and the day of the Tortoise's special flight, they gathered and donated wings to the Tortoise. They all took to the skies, together with their august guest, the Tortoise, who kept his plan close to his chest. When they arrived in Heaven, they were welcomed by servants and court jesters. Before their host introduced them to the reception area, the Tortoise convened a short emergency meeting with the birds and reminded them that their heavenly names were very important and they should memorise them.

The feast started with an opening speech by the Creator and he welcomed his guests a second time. He introduced them to a variety of food delicacies that was eye popping and an once-in-a-lifetime chance, much to the ecstasy of the Tortoise who was revelling in his devilish scheme. Then the Creator said,

"Kindly enjoy your first meal in my kingdom."

"My Lord, who owns these starters?" the Tortoise asked.

"All of you."

Delighted with the Creator's answer, the Tortoise took all of the starters and ate them for himself. The birds watched and waited in horror but stayed composed. The main dish was then served and the Tortoise again asked who owned the food. The Creator again answered, "All of you."

The Tortoise took the entire dish and began eating. Further horrified by what was happening and fearful that the Tortoise would finish the meal before they had the chance to have their share, the birds asked the Tortoise to pass the food round the table to everyone. Then the Tortoise asked them,

"Who owns the food?"

"All of us!" they replied.

"Well, my name is 'All of You' and so I own all the food presented here," he said. After saying this, he ate all the delicacies that were given to them by their host.

Meanwhile, the rest of the birds were left without any food. They made a decision that they would not take up a fight with the Tortoise because it might embarrass their host. The feast continued after the meal until the Creator announced that the feast was over. He thanked his guests for attending the party and wished them a safe return to earth and went back to his palace. When the birds arrived at the Port of Flight to return to earth, they took back their wings from the Tortoise to punish him for eating all the food that was served for everyone.

The Tortoise pleaded with the birds to pardon his selfish act but none of them accepted his apologies. They flew back to earth and he was left stranded at the Port of Flight. Trapped in the sky with no wings, he sent an SOS to his family on earth. He wrote that he was stuck in the heavens and needed them to gather soft material and clothing and place them outside so that he could land safely.

The SOS was intercepted by his enemies who made alternative preparations, including placing hard surfaces, knives and dangerous weapons on the open field where the Tortoise would land. When they were ready, they informed the Tortoise that everything was set for him to jump safe and sound to earth. The Tortoise was so happy and landed onto what he thought was a safe and secured area.

He crashed into the dangerous surfaces and sustained severe injuries; his whole scale was broken in several places and he was left unconscious. When his family heard what had happened, they rushed him to a Native Doctor who resuscitated him and patched his broken scales but was unable to return it to its original shape and form.

*   *   *

"My children," my grandfather concluded, "this is why the Tortoise has rough scales or looks patched. Also, I advise you all to learn from this story and never be greedy or betray the trust entrusted on you by others. You all will understand more about the story of the Tortoise when you grow up. Go to bed for I am done tonight."

6

The Lion and the Antelope

Once Upon a Time! In the Animal kingdom there were different species of mammals including reptiles and carnivorous animals that lived together. In this kingdom, the Elephant was the ruler and the Sub-Saharan Lion was the Opinion and Opposition Organiser. The Elephant ruled as a dictator and much to the dismay of other animals who organised a mass rebellion against him and ordered a new leadership election, led by the Lion.

The election campaign for a new leader of the Animal Kingdom went underway and the Lion took advantage of his position and strength to become a bully. He terrorised other animals and made it clear that, as leader of the rebellion he was going to be the next leader of the kingdom. The rest of the animals disagreed with him and decided that this would be tested in an election through secret voting.

By this time, the Lion was overtly confident that he was going to win the election because of his "outstanding contributions" to the *sunset days* of the Elephant's reign. He was very confident that instead of taking part in campaigns like his fellow contestants, he spent time preparing his inaugural speech. He met the Antelope who was one of the contestants and discouraged him from running as the new

Commander-in-Chief because of his meekness in nature and lack of charisma. He went as far as tr   and no animal would vote for him.

The Antelope did not feel downcast or threatened by the strength or threats of the Lion; instead, he intensified his election campaign, went from door to door, gatherings and organised events and delivered his manifesto, speeches and messages of good governance and an inclusive government. This paid off as his humility and manifesto attracted most of the smaller animals such as the Squirrel, Grass Cutter, and Fox to join forces to campaign to vote the Antelope as their new leader.

On Election Day, the Lion was convinced that he was the clear favourite and set up a committee to prepare his victory party. During this time, the Wolf, who was a secret supporter of the Lion and a returning officer, was chosen to announce the results of the votes at the Election Headquarter. When the results were handed to him, he opened the paper and discovered that the Lion had lost the election. At that instance, he contemplated putting the ballot papers back into the box but the fear that this could spark a revolt held him back. He also realised for the first time since the elections that he had lost all his powers and was no longer in a position to bully or dictate to other animals. Finally, he read the results and declared the Antelope to be the winner and the new leader of the Animal Kingdom. The win was a strong victory for the Antelope and his campaign manager, the Grass Cutter.

Triumphant celebrations erupted in the camp of the Antelope while the Lion became aggressive and turned to the one "buddy" he thought he had – the Wolf. He ran after him and pounced and deepened his paws into his skin and the Wolf fought back to defend himself. The fight that began because of betrayal turned to mayhem when other animals joined in the fight and the others took off from the Kingdom. The Elephant intervened to stop the fight but the Lion charged towards him and the Elephant flung him off with his tusk and dashed forward to kill him but was restrained by other big and stronger animals who were watching this royal rumble. Some of the animals whisked the Antelope away to an undisclosed location for protection while the rest of the smaller animals took off to avoid being "demolished" by the brutal Lion. The consequence of this pandemonium was lawlessness in the Kingdom.

Over at the undisclosed location where the new leader of the Animal Kingdom was seeking refuge, they continued their victory celebrations. When the festivities were over, the new leader and his campaign manager were retreating for the night and stumbled upon the Lion who was nursing his dislocated calf from the Elephant's pummelling. They mocked and jeered at him, taking the final result sheets that were in his hands and it dawned on him that he would never achieve the throne through greed and bullying. The Lion was ashamed and unable to fight back because of his injuries but assured the Antelope that as long as he was alive, he will fight back in due time and make sure that the Antelope never ruled the Animal Kingdom again.

In response, the Antelope and Grass Cutter told him this proverb: "When the Lion is down, an Antelope collects his debt."

7

Uyokanjo The Great Turtle

Once Upon a Time, in the village of Turtles. They believed in brotherhood and lived with rules and regulations. One of the rules was to vote for a new Head of the Clan when the former passed onto the Great Beyond. In this same village lived a turtle that was loved by most of her generation and neighbours. She was named Uyokanjo meaning, "Home" because of her rare qualities. She was brave, caring, strong and daring.

Before Uyokanjo was born, all animals lived together in the jungle as one big family. After her birth, she realised that although animals lived as one big family, the unit was not a happy one for the weaker, calmer and smaller size animals especially the Turtles. They were discriminated upon and continued to suffer intimidation, bullying, violence and sometimes death in the hands of bigger animals. This non-stop coercion made the Turtles to vow to reward anyone that came to their rescue.

At this time, the Bull was on a rampage and terrorising animal farms, barns and the entire Animal Kingdom. The Animal King sent out his hunters to capture the Bull but they were unable to capture the criminal. The king then made an appeal through his Town Crier that there would be a great reward to anyone who captured the Bull. The Town Crier went round the kingdom and announced the appeal of the King: "Hear this, all animals; the King has promised to grant any request to any animal that catches Bull the criminal."

Animals that heard the news passed it on from one animal to the other but none of them were courageous to plan a capture. They feared that the strength of the bull would have devastating consequences if they confronted him and this allowed the Bull to continue to run amok. Uyokanjo though thought of a plan to lure and capture the Bull, without the involvement of other animals.

While other bigger animals contemplated and mapped out ways to capture the Bull, Uyokanjo made her own plans. She went to the forest and dug a 7ft trench in the ground and disguised it with shrubs. After finalising her forest plan, she went to the Bull and convinced him to flee the Kingdom by using a safer road that she had discovered. Unaware of her arrangement, the Bull followed Uyokanjo to the forest and into her 7ft trench trap. She hurried back to the Kingdom to tell the King of the news.

When Uyokanjo was brought to the presence of the King, she told him that she had captured the Bull. After hearing the news, the King hailed Uyokanjo and without hesitation, he allocated more land for all Turtles as a reward for Uyokanjo's bravery. After rewarding Uyokanjo and the rest of the turtles, he said to everyone gathered around "what men can do, a woman can do better."

Uyokanjo went on to become a great female Turtle. She also became the new head of the clan in her community and throughout the kingdom.

8

The Lamb of God

Once Upon a Time! In the land of animals, everything was equal and all animals ate and worshipped together. Christianity was also at its pinnacle and there was no intimidation, bullying or violence and there was no such thing as survival of the fittest. On the contrary, animals loved one another.

As Christianity was top of their daily life and agenda, every animal went to mass and the Priest made sure that he acknowledged the presence of Chieftains before, and after mass. The Priest offered each Chieftain a handshake but never did same to rookies of the Club of Knights. One of the new recruits of the Club of Knights was Mr. Goat who bragged continually to his friends about his new status.

Bursting with self confidence about his new position, Mr. Goat invited Mr. Sheep, to come along and witness their celebration of mass. On the day of mass, they arrived late and when they entered the Church building, the Priest was presiding over the communion rite and saying: "Behold the Lamb of God who takes away the sins of the world, happy are we who are invited to his supper..."

When Mr. Goat heard this, he fumed and lamented to himself: "Goodness God, what is happening? How can the Priest recognise this poor Lamb who has never before set foot in this church?"

He was furious at what he believed was injustice to him, and swore to never return to any Church in Africa. Realising that the goats were no longer a part of their celebration, humans decided that they were the best animals to offer to Priests at the altar in Churches, thus they started offering goats to Priests on Sundays.

This angered the goats and every time they are brought down the altar, they are reminded of how they were unjustly treated by priests. It also explains why Goats scuffle and cry whenever they see an altar.

9

The Wise Ant

In the land of insects, there lived two friends, Locust and Soldier Ant, who shared one nest. They were fortunate in that they had abundant harvest because of heavy rainfall that blessed their land and made their farm crops to blossom. As a result, there was much to eat, drink, merry and enough to store for many months.

Just after the season's superfluous harvest, the Village Clairvoyant predicted that a great famine was going to strike and that it would last for two years because the gods of rain were directing the course of the rain to another planet for a more beneficial course.

When the Village Town-Crier heard this prediction, he went throughout the community, for many days, and warned everyone that there was a prophecy of a horrible famine to come. He advised everyone to "Store yams and food crops in their barns because teeth would be gnashed if people failed to do so."

The Soldier Ant called all his friends and asked them to assist him to store as much food as they could while they were waiting for the great famine. Whilst the Soldier Ant and his friends were loading their barns and houses, the Locust was occupied with merrymaking and eating and drinking and not stocking any excesses. The Soldier Ant saw this with great sadness and advised the Locust that to cut back in his choice of lifestyle. He warned him about the impending famine and told him to "save for the future because the strength of one's tomorrow lies in their actions today", he said. For the time being, the Soldier Ant continued stocking much food. He even dug underground holes and built mud-like hill houses at the top to store food. As predicted, the wave of famine struck with rancour and before too long, some of the insects, especially, the Locust, began to starve.

The vengeance of the famine persisted and the Soldier Ant started to face the risk of losing all his food reserves to other lazy insects. He fled from the village and went to live in his new underground home that was fortified, and also filled with food reserves. After he abandoned the village, the Locust was afraid that he was going to starve to death and started looting and stealing from other animals. The stock that the Locust stole, however, did not last long and he starved to death like a pauper, because of his laziness.

10

The Rejected Stone

There was once a rich woman named Nneka who was married to Okonkwo and they had two daughters. The first daughter was called Akwugo but her features had no resemblance to her father and or any member of his family. This discrepancy brought constant arguments between the couple, as Okonkwo believed that his wife conceived Akwugo from her lecherous ways with other men. Unfortunately, Okonkwo was unable to support his suspicions and fears with facts because the era had no DNA proof. Their second daughter, on whom there was no question of her paternity, was called Agwawumma and was born blind.

Before Nneka acquired her wealth, she lived with her husband, Okonkwo, until the Great War erupted and soldiers attacked their village and took away their possessions. During and after the war, there was widespread starvation and Okonkwo was no longer able to provide for his family and wife who was pregnant with their second child. His inability to provide for his family infuriated Nneka and she turned to infidelity and adultery with many solders.

She brought different men to her home and matrimonial bed and turned her husband into a servant who, on many occasions was molested and turned into a prisoner of war by her soldier boyfriends. As scarcity of food became endemic, she intensified her lecherous behaviour and bought into prostitution as a means of making money. She amassed a lot of wealth from this trade and became a woman of high status in the village. After a while, the war ended and it was at this same time that she gave birth to her second daughter who was born blind.

Nneka was intensely materialistic and treated her two daughters differently. While she loved her elder daughter who went into prostitution because she lavished her with gifts and money on daily basis, she disliked and disregarded Agwawumma the blind child because of her disability and inability to raise money from men.

Meanwhile, Okonkwo was unable to manage or bear this reprehensive crisis and abandoned his family and home and fled the village for a distant city. When he arrived in the city, he worked hard and became a successful contractor. After amassing much wealth, he returned to his village in search of his blind daughter although the thought of his family home always brought back "The Once Upon a Time Wife" memories.

He drove in his new car into his village and former home and it took his estranged wife and other people many hours to recognise him. At the same time, he was shocked by what he was seeing: the hand of time had caught up with his ex-wife and she became very poor. He met her by the roadside begging for food and money. In her arms was a starving son, on whose faith they both knew. Also by her side was Akwugo, her first daughter, "whose stomach stretched forward" - an indication of pregnancy.

Okonkwo was shocked by the sights of his ex-wife and "daughter" but felt no pity for them and demanded to see his blind daughter Agwawumma. His former wife apologised for her past mistakes and asked Okonkwo to take her back. The newly made wealthy man smiled at these thoughts and told her that he could never be with her again.

He took his blind daughter to the city and to a Traditional Healer who restored her sight and she was able to go to school and live a normal and happy life. She was well disciplined and intelligent and got married to a wealthy and lovely man. When her father passed over to the Great Beyond, she inherited all his fortune and expanded on her father's legacy.

11

Man Shall Not Live by Bread Alone

Prempe Ayew was born in Takoradi, Ghana, and had never travelled out of his country until December 2008, when his company rewarded his handwork with a paid holiday to the United Kingdom and the Republic of Ireland. He came from London to Dublin to spend some time with me in my humble residence. When he went back to his country, he wrote a letter to thank me for making his short holiday in Dublin very exciting. We maintained contacts and talked very often on diverse issues, including the 2008 elections in Ghana but of significant, was Prempe's discovery, in Europe, that he could solve the Biblical puzzle of 'Man shall not live by bread alone.'

Prempe is a practising Christian, like many Africans, and reveres the bible and is addicted to reading its passages. When we spoke over the phone, he said that he was very concerned by some of his experiences in the West, going from diminishing values of Christianity to food menus. He added that while in England and Ireland, he discovered that the Gospel of Mathew, 4:4 was written for Europeans and not for Africans, and that the discovery was crucial to his long time curiosity of the phrase in the bible that states that

"One does not live on bread alone but on every word that comes from the mouth of God."

Prempe told me that on his first day in London, he went out for breakfast and was served a small slice of bread and butter. The bread, he said, was as hard as bread exposed to the Harmattan wind at the Nigerian North West Trade Wind Centre. When he tasted the bread, he said he decided that he was not going to eat his share of the bread. When the second meal was brought to his table, it was still served with a slice of bread and much to his disappointment. After the second meal, he decided that out of respect for his host, he was not going to make any official complains about his dislike for the bread; rather, he was no longer going to eat bread.

On his second day, he was served bread sandwich for lunch and he refused to eat his meal. Still, he did not make any complains. Four days into his visit and four days of being served with plain hard bread and not eating it, Prempe said his host took notice that he was not eating his meals and changed his meal on the fifth day.

Hurray! He thought when he saw a different meal. He was served with a different type of bread – baguette and sandwiched with egg mayonnaise, ham and lettuce. This horrified him and he felt that the only escape was to tell his host that he does not take lunch. The next couple of days and meals saw different kinds of bread, from Bagels, Garlic, to Toasted Sliced bread and stuffed with sweet corn, bacon, smoked chicken and omelette. Still, the varieties failed to impress or arouse his appetite.

He told me that he then decided to go to restaurants, cafés and grocery outlets to find out if this was the trend. When he visited these places, he found out that there was bread everywhere and he stressed to me on the phone that "O Boy! Everywhere I went, I was very surprised that I was served bread as part of the menu."

He said that he was further horrified that when he came to Ireland the trend continued and it made him to come to the conclusion that the Holy Bible, as quoted in Mathew 4:4, was truly not written for Africans but for Europeans because although healing cometh by faith, bread is not a staple food in Africa. Thus, "Man shall not live by bread alone."

12

Why the Tortoise is Bald

Once Upon a Time! The King of the Jungle organised a big feast and invited all animals. The King had great love for lavished ceremonies and he organised extravagant functions every year, to commemorate his ascension to the throne. On these occasions, he offered his guests different kinds of foods, fruits, palm wine and spirits to show his appreciation for their support throughout the year. In return, his friends and well-wishers paid him respect by presenting him with well-known special gifts.

Among the animals invited to the annual great feast was the Tortoise who was noted for his love for hand-outs. He was clothed in a fanciful robe and hat, and set out with his friends to join the rest of the animals who had already converged to celebrate in grand style. On their way to the Jungle Square, they prided themselves in the quantity of food and drinks that they were going to consume because they were prohibited from taking food reserves from the venue. They planned that the next alternative to the prohibition was to "eat and drink till they dropped" at the square. (After the previous ceremony, the king placed an embargo that from oncoming years, no animal was allowed to take food or drink reserves away from the Jungle Square or the Kingdom.)

When the Tortoise and his friends arrived at the Jungle Square, they sat closest to where the foods and drinks were lined up, but his friends were unaware of his ulterior motives for wearing a hat. The first meal was served and it was maize meal with vegetable soup, and followed by other delicacies such as palm wine and yam porridge, which was the best and popular meal in the jungle. As this was a special dish, the tradition demanded that the yam porridge would always be served hot.

The Tortoise loved yam porridge and decided that he was going to hide some of the porridge in his hat even though it was very hot. Without wasting any time, he finished his first plate of the yam porridge and requested another. When the second plate was handed to him, he took the dish away from the table, to the side of the forest, and poured it on his head and covered it with his hat. He asked for the third plate and did same with it but the porridge was very hot and he began to feel unbearable pains. He requested to go home and said he was suffering from constipation. On his way from the Jungle Square, he ran fast in order to avoid being roasted by the hot porridge, underneath his hat.

When he arrived at his hut the pain was excruciating but he did not rush to remove his hat in the presence of his children. Rather, he went to the side removed the porridge with care in order to preserve the yam porridge stored underneath his hat on his head. After removing the porridge, he realised that all of his hair was burnt. This left him bald and explains why the Tortoise has a baldhead.

13

The Sacrificial Chicken

Once Upon a Time! In the jungle where animals lived very happily, animals began disappearing and ending up death without explanation. Some of the body parts turned up unexpectedly on shrines used by humans and this sparked speculations that humans were kidnapping and using animals for sacrifices to their gods.

These barbaric acts ignited an emergency meeting among all animals in the jungle. The day of the meeting coincided with the Annual Festival of Chicken, which proscribed them from leaving their jurisdiction. The feast was an age-long traditional reunion festival, and although Chickens were also victims of humans' malevolence, they could not trade their feast for the emergency meeting. So, they sent information to the other animals that they would not be attending the meeting because of their allegiance to their age long festival. The news enraged the rest of the animals and they made many appeals to the Leader of the Chickens to persuade his clan members to be at the meeting, but their requests were abortive.

When the day of the emergency meeting came, the Chickens were busy decorating and preparing their village for the festival. They ate and drank and partied into late hours of the morning and even set aside reserves for their fellow animals that were not at the emergency meeting. The other animals carried on with the emergency meeting and debated on what to do about the kidnappings and killings in the land.

In addition to finding a solution on the crisis, tempers "flew" about the absence of the Chickens at the meeting. The animals that disliked the Chickens and those that were against their absence spearheaded a campaign to punish the Chickens for their lack of cooperation. They plotted that, as punishment for their lack of representation, all Chickens should be offered to Humans as sacrificial meat and blood for their gods. This type of punishment was widely argued amongst the animals and when they failed to reach a compromise through balloting, they sent the case the Court.

At Court, it was decided that from that moment onwards, all Chicken were going to be used as human's favourite source of blood and meat for sacrifices to their deities. The Court also instructed the chickens to choose between leaving the jungle and living with humans, or, staying in the jungle and facing the wrath of other animals. When the Chickens were confronted with these choices, they felt that if they took the latter choice, it would be the worse of two evils because their fellow animals would prey on them. They then decided to escape the jungle to live with humans.

This explains why Chickens live with humans and why they are mostly used for meat and sacrifices to divine beings.

14

No Smoke Without Fire

Once Upon a Time! In the land of Ngooma, there was a successful hunter named Ikemefula. He had ten children, and slew more animals than all of his fellow hunters throughout his village and neighbours. He even singlehandedly killed a lion that had terrorised the village for many years. This act of bravery earned him the title of 'Ogbuagu', meaning "Lion Killer", the greatest honour for any member of his family to have received in over a hundred years. The title was so special that it was conferred on him by the elders of the Traditional Council, and his proficiency made many people to revere him, yet, created many enemies among his peer.

When Ikemefula was twenty-five years of age, he married Agbomma who bore him five children before accidentally drowning at Umungooma River, as she fetched water. He then got married to a second wife who was his dead wife's maid and a very attractive but controversial servant called, Adamma. She was rumoured to be wicked and despite all advices from Ikemefula's friends and family against marrying his onetime servant, Ikemefula went ahead and married her. They later had five more children.

One night Ikemefula went out to hunt for a Caracal and was struck in his eyes by a tree branch that left him instantly blind. Fortunately, he was out with his dog that was called "Anwu-Anwu", and he rushed to rescue him from the tree and then led him home. When they arrived in his compound, his family took him to Traditional Doctors for treatment but all attempts to heal him and recover his vision failed, and he became blind. Suddenly, life became difficult for Ikemefula and his peers, who were jealous of his achievements, were delighted about his mishap and failed to assist him.

For many months, he was unable to regain his sight and his wife, Adamma, became his main carer. However, Adamma quickly transformed from a caring and loving wife, to a neglectful wife and began to maltreat her disabled husband and his first five eldest children. She assigned them to take up the roles of maids and servants, and rationed their food portions. When this was not enough, Adamma started having sexual relationships with other men.

When she was confronted by her husband on these despicable changes, Adamma snapped back with hate and anger. Not willing to take any more instructions or criticism from her now disabled husband, she decided to do the unthinkable. She made up her mind to kill her husband so as to put an end to his confrontations.

Adamma poisoned her husband's food that was cooked by her second and favourite daughter from his first marriage. Ikemefula died a short time later and Adamma drove the orphans away from their family home into the streets.

Meanwhile, the life of a onetime proud and brave hunter and father was once again brought to an abrupt end by the iniquity of a woman.

15

Babatunde and the Beautiful Mermaid

Once Upon a Time! There was panic in the village of Kosofe, a tiny island in a Rainforest that was home to only fifteen kindred who were descendants of Sofe "The Warrior". Sofe was noted for having many wives and concubines and offspring. The number of offspring from his second generation were said to be as many as the eastern stars of the heavens. These descendants became renowned for fishing, palm wine tapping and intensive agriculture, which were earlier sources of their livelihood. It was, however, the art of tapping palm wine that catapulted the Kosofe people, who were also located within the Mbaa River that was under the Kingdom of Asante.

One afternoon, the most attractive female ever seen by the human eye emerged from the banks of Mbaa River, which provided the Kosofe people much significance, including water for cooking, drinking, and cleaning dishes, clay pots and other kitchen utensils. She covered her breasts with a raffia-like twined "bra" and had extremely long dark hair that fell to both sides of her sumptuous hips. She had what looked like a fish tail as she rose from beneath the depth of the waters and walked towards the people who had gathered for an afternoon chat.

Confusion and panic set in as people ran and headed in all directions of the village to report this unprecedented happening on the banks of River Mbaa. As they ran, a mother who was also at the shore of the river with her two toddlers, became consumed by freight and abandoned her tots and too off. The Mermaid walked up to the babies and took them in her hands and went back into the river from whence she disappeared.

The children were never seen again by any of the villagers but there were reports of several sightings of the mermaid sunbathing on the banks of the river. The appearance of the mermaid started a trail of disappearances in the village, and a woman who went to the river to clean her cassava fruits was never seen again. This was quickly followed by another mysterious disappearance of a maiden.

The misfortunes shattered the peace and tranquillity that had existed in the village for many years. It also cut off the main water source as people were terrified of what awaited them in the river if they went to fetch water. Fishermen and Palm Wine Tappers, who also used the river to gain access to the source of their produce, were left with no stock because they feared what lay inside or beyond the river.

As the community was grieving their losses, the council of elders met to decide how to face this threat "head-on". Believing in the adage that 'an elder cannot watch a goat give birth in a stead', the elders made a public announcement and offered a bounty reward to anyone who resolved the mystery. They added that "whoever solved the mystery, would name their interest".

(Oral History has it that for anyone to be able to catch a mermaid, they must possess strong spiritual and natural powers that include the power of wealth and affluence.)

The announcement, that an enormous reward would be given to anyone that captured the mermaid, turned the strongest wrestlers, palm wine tappers and palm fruit cutters into mermaid hunters. All of them set out to end the terror and win the prize and also get the pride that came with saving Kosofe Village from this monstrous creature. One of the men was called Babatunde and he was known to be one of the fiercest warriors to hail from Kosofe and was never beaten and or defeated in matches.

As a child, Babatunde inspected his father's palm wine, deep into the melancholy of the night, on the West side of the Mbaa River. He did this in the hours when no one, not even his father, was able to venture into the depths of darkness, let alone the deep creepy waters. Babatunde was so fearless that when he was thirteen years old, a sorcerer visited his mother and revealed that her only son had special gifts and was blessed by the gods. This revelation did not come as a surprise to her or her husband.

Babatunde, like most of the fine men involved in the hunting, searched for days with no results. Some of the men also vanished in the process and their bodies were never found. Babatunde became even more troubled by this development and set up a new plan that involved using his supernatural powers.

One night when everyone was asleep, he went to the banks of River Mbaa and sprinkled a slippery substance and retreated into the bushes and laid in wait for the beautiful mermaid. Suddenly, he saw a heavenly figure coming out of the water and walking towards the trunk of a tree. She started to sit on the trunk but accidently slipped and landed on the slippery surface and began struggling to get back on her feet.

Babatunde took advantage of that moment and rushed forward and grabbed her tightly from the back around the neck and making it difficult for the mermaid to resist. The mermaid let out an eccentric scream for help and two giant bats landed on Babatunde out of the blue, and he struggled to maintain his grip while also crying out for help. Then an old woman with beads and cowry shells adorned on her neck, waist and wrists, appeared and battled the bats away and allowed Babatunde to break free from their grips. He dragged the beautiful mermaid to the village square and screamed to the four corners of the village that he had captured the fiend.

The people of Kosofe woke up in the wee hours of the night to the sound of conquer and conquest from Babatunde and into a new dawn of a free and peaceful village. Festivities started and Babatunde was crowned a Chief and given all his demands in compensation for his act of valour. The mermaid later lost her powers and could no longer return to the river world and Babatunde got married to her and they lived happy ever after.

16

The Meaning of Harvest Thanksgiving

In parts of Africa, Harvest Thanksgiving, code name "The Festival of Harvest", means "loads" of celebrations in thanksgiving to a Supreme Being. The festival takes place at the beginning of the year, after a successful planting season.

In the medieval days, masses took religion as a central part of their daily lives. They celebrated yearly harvests through a festival in which they thanked different deities for awarding them with successful harvests, prosperity and protection. They also used the festival of harvest to exhibit their farm products, which were presented for blessings in the place of worship of the Creator.

However, when Christianity penetrated the interiors of Africa, all facets of the people's ways of life was affected, causing social disorder. Colonial masters used treaties and false promises of fair trade and protection to exploit and export raw material from within the rich interiors of Africa. As the colonial masters took control of the lives of the local people, they also introduced them to Christianity that usurped some local values and traditions.

Colonialism soon spread like wildfire into the psychological terrain of man in Africa and before too long, the new religion wrestled the Africans' gods and traditional ways of life and many festivals replaced their introductory rites with those of the newly introduced ways of Christianity.

Families began to burn objects and symbols of deities that they prayed to, and villages and communities sacrificed their ancestral shrines and replaced them with churches that were set up by European messengers of Jesus Christ. Gradually, Africans embraced this new way of worship and also discovered that they could seek solace in Christianity.

As Christianity continued to grow, the scope of the festivities of The Harvest Festival widened and changed to suit western ways. The blood and sacrificial rituals that happened in shrines were wiped out and other aspects were accepted in Church. In this new form of celebration, new converts brought farm harvests to present to God as a mark of their conversion of faith. This new way of celebrating the Festival of Harvest has continued to this millennium and different forms also continue to emerge.

One of the new forms of "The Festival of Harvest" is called "The New Yam Festival". Some ethnic groups, especially the Igbo people of Nigeria, also celebrate it in the West. In Ireland, the Igbo celebrate The New Yam Festival without animal and church sacrifices, and while most of the traditional rites are no longer performed, it still contains minor traditional rituals such as the pouring of libation and incantation. The eldest in the group only ever performs this part of the festival.

Another example of a contemporary festival of harvest is one that happened in St Peter's Church, Phibsboro, D7,

Dublin, on the 14th September, 2008, and unlike in the olden times where people brought gifts and harvests that depicted their works to the Church service, this type of celebration comprised people who showcase their traditional African regalia and donated alms. This new kind of festival has become a yearly event and demonstrates the riches that Africans possess and also the changing patterns of African culture

Even though the system of celebration has wavered and the worship of Jesus Christ continues to gather momentum, some aspects of the culture are still strong and are still being enacted to mark the true and original meaning of harvest thanksgiving.

17

The Armed Robber and the Gate of Heaven

Once Upon a Time! A great famine struck the Animal Kingdom after a draught caused serious damages to land and food crops. This saw a shortage of food supplies and bullying among animals while carnivorous animals that were starving started to kill and eat smaller animals. After a while, the harassments and killings stopped and animals started to change their ways in order to guarantee a place in heaven.

Suddenly, a new wave of lifestyle erupted where animals began to bow to the ways of Christianity and virtue, and there was an even bigger frenzy to go to heaven. They attended church services in big numbers and vowed to keep the Ten Commandments as instructed by the God of Jacob.

They also began to shun social ills, like what happens in most conservative societies, even though they were undergoing acute hardship and famine. They replaced social ills with hard work and brotherly love for one another and saw this new way of life as the gateway to heaven where everything was said to be in abundance for those who avoided evil. Meanwhile, those who indulged in sin, no matter how trivial it was, were said to be going to hell.

The Hyena was the most popular animal in the Animal Kingdom but hardly participated in community work and did not believe that going to church would get any animal into heaven. He told other animals that in order for them to go to heaven they had to have certain qualities, which included strict discipline and abstinence from greed and hypocrisy.

It should be noted, however, that the Hyena was a notorious robber and waited on bush paths to waylay animals. He committed the crimes outside his local area where none of the other animals that knew him could recognise him. As such, he kept a clean profile in his kingdom and even enrolled to assist the security team, but as the adage goes that "there is no secret beneath the sky", some of his relatives and friends knew of his criminal record but were tight lipped about it.

One day the Hyena and his gang of thieves received a tip-off about some wealthy traders who were going on a business trip in a nearby kingdom. The gang was informed that the wealthy whole-sellers were carrying large sums of money with them and were travelling without members of their security team. Meanwhile, the traders were unaware that their movements had been divulged by one of them and so set out without any member of their security team. The Lion and Tiger were members of their security team but refused to accompany them because they were demanding for better wages. Previously, the Lion and Tiger protected them by fighting off attackers and ensured that the traders had a swift and smooth trade and felt that they deserved better pay for their work.

As the traders were aware that they had no security team with them, they took a different route with hopes that it was safer and more secured from robbers. This was, however, not the case as a short time into the detour they were ambushed by raiders. The raiders wore balaclava over their faces and took away their bags of cowry and important and expensive belongings and abandoned them in the forest with nothing. This left the traders in shock and fear and marked the end of their business trip.

Among the traders were Mr Dog, Duck and Chameleon. When they were ambushed, Mr. Chameleon reacted very quickly and dashed into the bush with his money before the robbers had the chance to attack him. Unfortunately, Mr. Dog and Duck were not lucky and collapsed to the ground and died of heart attacks once the raiders left. In his hiding place, Mr. Chameleon was able to recognise the distinct voice of the Hyena instructing the traders to empty their bags.

Back in the Animal Kingdom, the world came to an end and a scramble began among animals who wanted to go to heaven. Some of them were happy and comfortable that they would be going to heaven because by their estimation, they had done everything right and deserved a place in heaven. The animals were selected into three groups: the first group composed of those that were legible to enter heaven while the second group was going to purgatory and the last group was going to hell. On the holy gate of heaven, where flats were being shared to those who made it, the Hyena stood as the controller and was ushering the selected few to go in.

Some of the animals who recognised Mr. Hyena from his fraudulent lifestyle were shocked to see him controlling the gate of heaven and murmured among themselves that the gate they were standing on was the wrong one. "No way, this must be a wrong direction because I know that gateman. He is a thief," Mr. Chameleon fumed. "That bastard is a criminal; definitely this place is hell or purgatory'. Another retorted.

"My children, I tell you today that if you want to go inside the bus, you should never look at what is written on the body of the bus. Mr. Hyena was a notorious robber but he regretted his actions and repented yesterday, with his whole heart, soul and body", St. Peter said as he came out of the golden door.

"The kingdom of God is like the parable of the Lost Sheep in which the Sheppard lost one of his hundred sheep but went in search of it; the last shall always be the first', he added.

After looking at themselves with utmost scrutiny, they moved in.

18

The Soured Soup

Once Upon a Time! There was a widow in a village named Binin-kebbi. Her name was Agama Lizard and she lived with her five children in a double attached underground tunnel, besides the only rabbit that was left in the village. The rabbits had been forced to abandon all their belongings in search of refuge in other villages when a mass action was launched against them. The other animals then looted and took ownership of all their belongings and Mrs Lizard was one of the animals that also benefitted from the abandoned belongings. When the only rabbit that was left in the kingdom died, she again occupied his home and all his lands.

Mrs. Lizard became very wealthy and fortified her new home that was snake-shaped in nature and had one conventional entrance to the front and two covert let out doorways in the back, which served as emergency exits in the case of attacks from predators. For security reasons, Mrs. Lizard and her family, like many underground reptiles, always blocked the corridor to the main lobby and she instructed her five children that this was not going to change especially, when she was not at home.

One day, she gathered her children and informed them that she was travelling to her birth place for the burial ceremony of her uncle. She told them that they were going to be on their own and that they should take care of the home. Before she left them, she cooked a big pot of mushroom soup that she anticipated would serve them for seven days, which was the duration of her absence. When she left, the boys started having differences and arguments over rights and responsibilities, so much so that, no one did anything and the house became untidy. Also, they left the mushroom soup without heating for days.

On another day, while they were arguing over who would heat the soup for their meal, they received a visitor. It was their mother's sister who came in bearing a message. She informed them that their mother was killed in an ambush around her place of birth. As a result, things were no longer going to be the same and each of them had to carry out different responsibilities, she said.

The last son immediately volunteered that he would be responsible for the house chores and started by heating the soup. As he heated the soup over and over again, he found that the soup was sour and that no amount of re-heating would bring back the original taste of the soup. Even though he was unable to change the sour soup, his brothers applauded his good intention and this gave him an edge over his four elder brothers and they choose him to lead the family in domestic chores. He was also chosen to be the mediator whenever they had differences.

None of them, however, remembered to keep the door blocked, which was their mother's N° 1 priority. Then one night, they had their first test while they were asleep. The Green Snake heard that Mrs. Agama was dead and that her children were on their own and went to their house to devour them.

The last son heard a noise coming from the lobby and was disturbed by it and woke up quickly. He went to the corridor and moved the pebbles and locked the lobby just like his late mother had instructed them and before the intruder completed his mission. This saved them from a calamity that would have wiped out their entire household. When his brothers woke up, he told them what had happened and they hailed him for being a hero.

Part Two: Short Stories

1

McDowell and The King

Once Upon a Time! There lived a King in the land of the Penguins, located off the Coast of Africa. He was a wealthy, popular and powerful King and narratives about his might spread far beyond his kingdom. He was also a wise King and this gave him the supremacy to arbitrate in disputes that were faced by animals. At this time, there were many disputes faced by Squirrels especially during the period of Harmattan and autumn in Africa, and the wise king always resolved them.

In this kingdom, the custom demanded that the King got married to a new wife every two years. As a result, female Penguins lobbied and even set up schemes so as to become the King's new wife. Some of the female Penguins were noted to scheme their ways into the King's heart by plotting to kill his other wives in order to take their places.

In this Kingdom also lived a poor orphan Penguin called McDowell. His parents died when he was young and his family members confiscated all their properties and forced him to grow up miserably. He faced mistreatment and rejection from other Penguins and did not belong to any association. For most of his life McDowell survived by scavenging on debris and receiving alms from passers-by.

One day, something terrible happened, and the King summoned all the members of the Penguin Lords' Council to announce it. "Brethren, I have lost my majestic ring, therefore, the kingdom will have to be searched," the King said.

The members of the Penguin Lords Council were horrified by this revelation and one of them said to the King: "May your majesty, reign long. When and where did this happen?"

Not willing to give out the details of the missing ring, the King told them in a commanding tone: "Please, inform the town criers to announce the loss of my diamond ring. Also tell them to inform every penguin that there would be a great reward for anyone that found the ring. The penguin that finds it will rule over one of my vassal states. If it is a male penguin that finds it, I will also give him my beautiful daughter to become his wife, which is my greatest gift", the King ended.

"The king's wish shall be done; his majesty's words shall be done", the Lords of the Council responded.

Town criers went to all corners of the Kingdom and announced that the King's special ring was missing. They assured penguins that the King promised to reward anyone that found the ring. This message was disseminated around the kingdom and every Penguin joined the search for the coveted ring. They hoped that if they found the ring they would also receive good tidings that were attached to it. Some members of the Penguin Lord's Council also forced their offspring to join the search so that a find would boost their relationship with His Royal Highness.

The pauper Penguin, McDowell, however, feared that other Penguins would harass him if he joined the search for the King's missing diamond ring and instead continued to search for food. After two weeks of frenzy searches, none of them found the ring and they started to lose hopes of ever recovering it, while, the King panicked over the possibility that the ring could never be recovered.

An Asian Vulture gave the Majestic Ring to the King and it contained some diabolic powers that could make the King to disappear in times of danger. Once the King put on the ring, he had the powers to travel without being seen, to all parts of the world. The ring also allowed him to belong to countless worldwide organisations, including the Penguin Witches Network. These details though were not known to other Penguins, not even to the members of the Council of the Lords of Penguins.

As the search teams failed to recover the ring, the Council Lords and subjects appealed to the King that they were going to buy him a new ring. Confused but tactical, the King accepted the request, at the same time, he increased the reward on whomever found the ring.

On a certain night, long after the search had failed to unearth the ring and the King was squirming in panic over the loss, McDowell went out to scavenge for snails. He picked up three medium seize snails and then was distracted by some weird noise. He looked towards the source of the noise and he saw a sparkling, like a star, and bent down to take a closer look but his beak got bunt, forcing him to retreat.

Reflecting on what to do, he decided that he would not give up the search for the source of the sparkle. He bent down further and saw that the source was a ring – a diamond ring, perhaps what every Penguin was searching for. McDowell picked up the ring and as he walked away, a crack voice emerged from the ring saying: "Please, say what you need and take me to the King; just say it! Just say it!"

The voice kept repeating the lines and McDowell decided to give in with a demand for food. Before he could finish his demand, dishes of delicious meals, including desert and nutritious drinks that were only served to the Penguin King appeared in front of him. He sat down by the bush side, shielded himself from any Penguin who could attempt to rob him of this opportunity and ate his entire meal. He then set out towards the King's Palace and when he approached the King's Guards, they were reluctant to let him in until he told them that he had found the King's Special Missing Ring.

Immediately, the guards allowed him into the palace and ran towards the King's Chamber. They shouted in ecstasy that the King's ring had been found. When the King heard the screams, he came out and confirmed that the ring McDowell found was his special ring. He then called for a celebration and rewarded McDowell accordingly. He also warned other penguins of the consequences of a conspiracy against McDowell, as some members of the Lords' Council had begun to stir wiles.

Like the great King that he was, the Penguin King kept to all his promises including a state organised wedding for his daughter and McDowell. "Stay with him for life as a real Penguin does" he said to his daughter and gave her in matrimony to McDowell.

McDowell became the King's closest confidant and rose from grass to grace.

2

The Careless Mother

In the land of Umuguma, there was once a woman who gave birth to a new baby – a boy. The woman had prayed and longed for a baby boy for many years but kept on having female children. When her family members and neighbours heard the news of her new bundle of joy, they were overjoyed that her longing for a male child had finally been answered. They visited her to pay their respects on her new achievement.

However, her friends and family were quick to advise her to cut back on the number of hours that she spent in the farm. The woman was noted for spending long hours on the farm, together with her young children and never took time to rest. Some of her neighbours even said that she left the house as soon as the Cockerel heralded a new dawn and only returned at sunset. There were also reports by medical practitioners that she never took their advice of resting and that this happened throughout all her pregnancies.

When her baby was just two months old, she again ignored warnings from medical experts and friends, and started going to the farm. She took her last daughter each time she went to the farm so that she could look after the baby while she worked on the cassava farm. As the tot was eight months old, she took him and her ten-year old daughter to a very far distant farm. The farm was once a forest and was home to many dangerous animals and reptiles, but once deforestation took place, locals began t cultivate it for food crops. As she went to the farm, she took "home-made grinded cassava soup and dried cassava" to feed the baby because he had refused to eat before they left the house

When they arrived in the farm, she left her daughter and son, about three hundred metres away from where she was working so that they would not distract her. She asked her daughter to try to see if the baby would eat: "Keep trying if he will eat", she said, and left them. She went with her hoe and cutlass to cultivate the soil but after about one hour, she heard her daughter screaming:

"Mama! Mama! It is swallowing so slowly"

"That is interesting, let it swallow", she shouted back to her daughter.

"Mama! Mama! Mama! It is really swallowing", the little girl raged and shouted, traumatised by what she was seeing.

"Please I need peace in this farm, let it swallow."

The little girl was shocked and started crying and running towards her mother. At that moment, the addicted farmer rushed to her daughter, who, by this time was too shaken to speak. She then ran over to where her son was supposed to be. What greeted her was a scene of incredulity and terror as she saw a python swallowing the last remains of her beloved son. She ran back home with her daughter, crying and blaming herself for allowing this to happen and not listening to warnings from family members and friends.

3

Dads are always Genius

Recently, I stumbled upon one of my high school classmates on the Internet, many years after we had separated. He was also my friend and serve in the US Marine. He left Nigeria with his mother for the United States of America in the late 1990's when his mother won the American Green Card Lottery.

My friend and I went to the Seminary and during our time there, our lecturers taught us about the importance of living together in a community and as one big family. This allowed us to spend time in recreational rooms where we made and shared jokes. Often, we talked about events that happened in our different homes, some of which were lies but we enjoyed them so we kept on telling them.

As soon as my US Marine friend and I re-united on the Internet, we talked about some of our old school stories and experiences, and I found that we still had the same nostalgia for our past. I reminded my friend of a joke that I regularly used on him in our school days. The joke was about his father and although we found it to be funny, we also knew that the content was real and that his story was not particular to only him and that it had negative impacts on the lives of many children in Africa. Unfortunately not much is spoken about it and so change cannot be effected.

In most parts of Africa, Fathers or Dads or Daddies are considered as intelligent and smart in all ramifications. They are mostly the breadwinners of families and are given credits when households thrive. Mothers, on the other hand, perform domestic chores, resolve family crises, look after children's general welfare and their behaviours, and are held responsible for the failure of the family unit.

Interestingly, I have never come across any dad that is not said to be academically intelligent. While growing up, I was made to believe that in the olden days, male children always came top in exams. If they failed their exams or other competitions, they were punished, and their mothers were blamed and scolded for their poor educational grades. Often, mothers were even blamed for passing their unintelligent (brainless) genes to their children. In the case where the children were exceptionally talented in school works and competitions, they earned titles, new names and accolades that portrayed similarities to their fathers. At the same time, the fathers were praised with outstanding hyperboles for their intellectual genes and the wonder is, this trend still goes on.

The classmate, who is still a friend of mine and who went on to become a US Marine was not a bright student in school. He always got the overall average that kept him out of expulsion; still, his father was never satisfied with him. His father insulted him with words that could cause a stroke to a septuagenarian and threatened, on several occasions, to remove him from school to become a Shoe Cobbler's apprentice. (It is worth noting that in most parts of Africa,

Shoe Cobblers are looked down as people with fewer opportunities and ambitions, as a result, people work very hard so as not to find themselves in this heavily prejudiced group of workers.)

During one Christmas holiday, my friend's father punished him yet again for his poor grades. He whipped my friend with a cane and asked him to kneel down for hours. While my friend went through his sentence, his dad lamented: "I still can't figure out where you got these poor genes from. None of my classmates were my match; Honestly, I still find your mum responsible for your dullard brains." In this case, my friend's chastisement lasted until a visitor intervened and secured his release.

One night while my friend and his family were moving to a new home in the outskirts of the town, he was responsible for sorting paperwork. His mother instructed him to keep valuable documents and set the rest aside for burning. His mother had fixed a blazing fire outside the house and was burning unwanted rubbish. As he sorted the documents, he came across many important ones but one certificate in particular caught his attention. It was one of his father's certificates.

"God Almighty, my Father graduated with third class honours from the University?" He exclaimed. Unable to believe what he was reading, he searched harder among the certificates and came across his Father's Leaving Certificate Record. To his horror; his Father took the exams a record number of four times before passing and completing the necessary requirements to guarantee him a place in the university.

After he absorbed what he had just discovered, he ran to his siblings and showed them the certificates he had found. The certificates were confirmations that their father was, after all, not the most intelligent man he had made himself to be. As facts are incredibly stubborn and difficult to erase, the children formed a group and marched hand in hand to their mother singing:

"The Genius Dad has been a fake one" they chanted and waited for their dad to return home.

4

Spare Caution and Spoil The Child

I was walking down Summer Hill Road to my friend when I heard ranting from a tiny voice behind me:

"Fucking Black Man, go back to your fucking country, you do not belong here"

When I looked behind me, I was shocked to find that the obscene words were coming from a little girl who could have been only four or five years old and whom I thought was a toddler to know the ABC of abuse and hate in a globalising society. Although I was unable to believe what I was witnessing, I managed a smile in a bid to dissuade the little one from continuing:

"How are you doing?" I asked the little girl, still trying to deter her from being obnoxious.

"Don't fucking talk to her, you fucking ..." A woman's voice joined that of the little girl.

I thought her to be the mother of the girl.

The woman and her daughter continued to insult me, while I decided to walk faster in order to disappear from their sights and from their verbal tirade. Even as I hastened my steps upfront, I could still hear the sweet tiny voice repeating the insults of her M'aa. Finally, I crossed the Summer Hill side of the Annesley Bridge, which overlooks parts of Croke Park, and could no longer hear their spitefulness. At last, I was out of the debacle.

As humorous as this incident was, it brought back memories of a sad story that I was told many years ago. It has been engraved on my memory ever since.

When I was ten years old, the Military Juntas ruled my beloved country, Nigeria. They enacted decrees upon decrees, one of which was for a Special Armed Robbery Tribunal (SART) that punished criminals for their offences.

One criminal who deserved punishment for his atrocities in the neighbourhoods, which left many people and families heartbroken was nicknamed "Terminator" alias "King of Night". The "Terminator" embarked on an indiscriminate killing spree, instilled fear in people, created a phobia for the night and turned wedding feasts to mourning scenes, yet, eluded the Cops for many years. It became known to the local people that "the fear of the Terminator was the beginning of life."

Retribution was on the way when the Terminator (AKA) King of Night, spearheaded a bank robbery and made away with millions of Nigerian Naira while also leaving five staff members dead. This was the epic of their carnage and made newspaper front pages across the country. The Terminator, however, was a different kind of armed robber in his underworld gang. He was a celebrated armed robber and his arrest would be a lottery for the newly formed SART who hoped that cracking the Terminator down would dissuade his followers.

Reacting to this grand theft, SART issued an unprecedented arrest warrant in the history of the state. The

Terminator was finally caught while attempting to smuggle himself out of the country, and six of his gang hoodlums were also later caught. The Head of SART promised that a tribunal was going to be held and heavy statements would be executed to serve as a warning to others.

Three weeks after the thieves were caught, the tribunal found the Terminator and his six accomplices guilty of grand theft and murder. The court sentenced the thieves to death by firing squad and set the location for the firing squad at Agwuishi Beachside Venue. Locals were invited to bear witness to the executions.

My uncle and I were among the mammoth crowd at the execution scene, waiting in anticipation and apprehension. We arrived at the scene thirty minutes early so as to be in plain view of what was going to ensue. A short time later, a Police Black Van, popularly known as the "Black Maria", pulled up with the damned criminals. As they disembarked, their executioners marched in rehearsal while a Priest lurked around with a Holy Bible and a Stole around his neck, waiting to hear their last confessions and to deliver the Sacrament of Extreme Unction.

The Terminator lined up and stood tall, even taller than ever seen, and with a Holy Rosary around his neck. He appealed to talk with his mother who was among the crowd. His mother walked up to his beloved son in shame, carrying a handkerchief in her hands, her face wet with tears, and the crowd looked on at the unfolding drama in silence. As she drew up closer to her son, she leaned towards him and brought her ear up to his mouth to hear his last words. What pursued was a terrifying and anguish cry from his mother as her very own beloved son chopped off her ear with his scissor teeth. The crowd withdrew in panic and frantic calls were made for the medics, while the Terminator shouted back at the crowd: "Do you know why I bit her ear off?"

"No!" The crowd screamed

The Terminator responded: "Thou it is too late to tell my story but I want you all to know that my mother taught me how to steal. All my life, she inspired me to steal, and unlike other good mothers, she kept all that I stole, including money, and even procured 'voodoo charms' for me so that they could protect me against being caught. With her, I came to know that when you spare the rod, you spoil the child", the Terminator concluded.

The last words of the Terminator were followed by the last blessings of the Priest and what came next were fire guns upon fire guns and this obliterated the terror and reign of the King of Night and his gang.

5

How important are Moonlight Games

In most parts of Africa, proverbs or wise sayings are an important part of gatherings of elders because they signify strength, wisdom and worth of the speaker and his/her speech. My grandfather once told me that "proverbs are like palm oil, which we use to eat words" and also that "proverbs expose words, as pregnancy tells the bitter truth, which a teenage girl finds hard to hide."

Not only are proverbs an important part of Africa, the climatic conditions also provide many opportunities. In mainland Africa and other rural areas, the tropical climate provides night time opportunities for children to listen to folktales from their grandparents, while the full moon also allows children to indulge in outdoor games. These traditions of moonlight storytelling and outdoor games have now been noted as helping to take away the stress of other unfortunate things that engulf most of Africa such as dictatorial regimes.

While I believe that children in Africa swim in this affluence of stories and weather, and nightmares of poorer lifestyles, children in the West lack quality time that allows for stories to be passed onto them. During the winter, I see kids in the West with winter clothing weighing almost more than their body weight and I wonder how they play happily in these coats in the winter, autumn and spring?

As these thoughts came to my mind, I took a walk to meet a friend of mine in the city centre of Dublin. While I stood with my hands astride my chest beside a wall on the walkway of Parnell Street in Dublin, I thought of my ESB letter that came in earlier from the post and then, I was distracted by a woman struggling to put her three playful kids into her car. This immediately reminded me of my moonlight games in Africa when I was like the kids. The most popular and my favourite game still remain The Hide and Seek Moonlight Game.

The Hide and Seek Moonlight Game can be played in two ways although they both have the same aim. The first type involves one pursuer and the pursued, which can be many people. To start the game, a lot is cast so as to get the first pursuer. This is followed by the most important part of the game where the pursuer chases his playmates in an attempt to find his replacement.

This involves a lot of running, following, listening and paying attention to tiny details of breathing from hideouts, in order to catch the next pursuer. Here, family houses, yam barns are some of the places that provide excellent and popular hide outs, especially in the rural areas that still have traditional ways of life and a lot playing space. The bright moon also makes it easy for the pursuer to easily find his next replacement.

The second type of "The Hide and Seek Moonlight Game" has the same target as the first but has a different manner in which the pursuer goes after his playmates.

A piece of cloth is used to blindfold the pursuer before he begins his chase of the next victims. Also, this is mostly played in the urban and city areas where there are no farms, yam barns or spacious areas and the playgrounds are smaller and restricted, thus easier to manage.

What makes the latter meaningful and attractive is that it allows children that are disabled to participate in the game. There is less running involved; instead, the blinded pursuer is taunted and whistled at and dared to get hold of the pursued. Also, as the playground is small and restricted, the number of participants is limited and when the pursuer catches his replacement, he removes his blindfold and blindfolds the new pursuer.

Like many other games, the hide and seek moonlight game kept us busy and happy, especially during the moonlight period when we played until the late hours of the night instead of eating and going to bed as some other children did. We became attached to these games that we failed to do our household chores and our parents scolded us for it. Unfortunately, we were never privileged with the policy of "spare the rod and spoil the child" and even after our parents scolded us, they also punished.

Reflecting on the mother and her three kids, I thought that some of these games could prove useful to children born in Europe because my experiences of both urban and rural lifestyle were diverse and rich, even more so with the opportunity of moonlight games.

As I contemplated these thoughts, I heard shouts of Goodbye! Goodbye! Bye! Bye! See you later. That brought me back to the present and back to Parnell Street where I realised with astonishment that the same kids that had provoked my memory of moonlight games were waving at me as their mother slowly drove away and disappeared into the busy night of Dublin City.

6

The Consequences of Lies

This story is about a friend of mine, Osei who met Yvonne and fell in love with her and dreamed for a long time of getting together with her. Osei met Yvonne at the Spirit Night Club on Abbey Street in Dublin, on one Saturday night. On this night, Yvonne had just split from her boyfriend and was out for a laugh with her friends. She was an extremely beautiful girl and like many other boys in the nightclub that night, Osei found her very attractive.

Struggling through the crowd, Osei moved closer to her on the dance floor and started hovering around her like a cockerel would do to a hen. He finally got his chance to dance with the beauty and the music instantly changed to the Hip Hop sounds of Snoop Doggy Dogg and much to his delight. They danced for the rest of the night and when the DJ announced at 2:20am that it was the end of the nightclub, Osei was disappointed that the night had come to a quick end. However, before he went home, he asked the beauty for her name and telephone number. When Yvonne read out her telephone number, he pulled his Samsung mobile phone and dialled the number to check that it was an authentic number. Satisfied that the number was working and was hers, Osei walked home feeling proud of his achievement.

Osei comes from Kumasi in Ghana and came to settle in Ireland a few months ago. When he arrived in Ireland, he picked up a job as a Street Vendor for the Evening Herald Newspaper, on the BallsBridge area in Dublin and rode a fairly used bicycle to commute the city centre from his home. As he struggled to earn his daily bread, he kept contacts with Yvonne who also maintained the contacts. As loquacious as he is, he said soft and romantic things to Yvonne and began talking his way into her heart.

Osei told his dream girlfriend that he is from Uganda and told her several lies including why he came to Ireland, even including his real name. In addition, he told Yvonne that he was a prince and that his grandfather was the infamous Idi Amin, former President of Uganda. Yvonne bought into what she thought was a genuine "fella", a Prince of Uganda and took a lot of interest in him.

Their friendship progressed on the mobile network and they set up a date to meet at 6pm, at the Spire on the O'Connell Street in Dublin. They planned to go for a drink and get to know each other better. On the appointment day, Yvonne arrived first at the base of the monument and waited for her new Prince. Meanwhile, it was at this time that Osei was finishing his vendor job, and had to cycle for fifteen minutes before getting to the appointment with Yvonne.

Cycling into the city, he realised that he was late and telephoned Yvonne to apologise for the delay. He told her that before he left the house, he picked the wrong wallet that contained large euro bank notes, and there was no change for them. So, he was searching for a parking space for his car so as to avoid the notorious city centre car clampers.

Osei decided that in order to avoid further delays and a possibility of being caught out, he would use a side road that was just off the O'Connell Street. As he negotiated the bend, something remarkable happened. He saw Yvonne and her friend from a distance as they stood at the entrance of a Spar Shop. He immediately climbed down from his bicycle to avoid being seen, and walked over to them. Unknown to him, Yvonne had seen him, and although she was shocked to see Osei on a bicycle, she decided to keep it discreet until after her friend left.

"Hello, Aminu", Yvonne greeted.

"Hi Pretty One", Osei answered. Appointment

After they had exchanged pleasantries and Yvonne's friend had left, "Aminu" began a litany of excuses on his lateness. As he made the excuses, he witnessed in agony as a man took his bicycle and pedalled off, but because he had told Yvonne many lies, he became too paralysed with embarrassment to go after the thief.

Yvonne, however, had witnessed the "Aminu Episodes" with interest and asked Osei why his face suddenly looked sad and pale. Osei turned back to Yvonne and looked at her with shock expression on his face. He replied that he had no reason to be sad, especially in the company of a very pretty woman, and touching her. Later, he admitted that he had divided thoughts and one was about some money transfer that he had made to his friend in Ennis, Co. Clare, before coming out to the appointment.

Then he received an even bigger shock when Yvonne walked away saying: "Go and get yourself a new bike, you fucking bullocks".

Finally, my friend Osei lost both his dream girl and his most treasured property on the Island of Ireland.

7

The African Grammarian

There was once a man who loved speaking English in a full-seize manner. His name was Kavubu, and he attended Teachers Training College, Kampala, during the departure of British Colonial Administrators. He went on to achieve the London GCE and Kampala TTC Certificates, and went from one rank to the other and later as a Head Master of an elementary school.

Mr. Kavubu's fondness for big grammar was as popular to residents of Kampala, as Podge and Rodge are to Irish viewers. After gaining admiration for his "knowledge and big use of grammar", Mr. Kavubu also earned the status of the best secretary in town, and many associations scrambled to employ him as secretary. As he was accepted as an erudite, he dealt with issues that affected the community in a manner that he saw best fit. At the same time, his command of the language intimidated local people and made them afraid to challenge him for fear of "being rubbished" and "swallowed" by what they thought were orthodox words.

One day while he was fast asleep, he was woken by the smell of smoke and realised that fire was consuming his flat. He hurried out of bed and went to his phone and called the

Fire Department. He shouted in a mimicked British accent: "Gentlemen, a conflagration of fire is consuming my magnificent edifice, please, accord me succour."

The firemen asked him to repeat what he said. He repeated the same thing. The men did not understand what he said and hung up the phone and went back to what they were doing. Whereas the men went back to work, Mr Kavubu waited for them to turn up to rescue his property that was melting into charcoal. When no one turned up, he dialled the emergency line again and said: "Gentlemen, fire is razing down my house, please, come and help me."

"Ok! We will be there very shortly", the receiver answered.

As promised, the fire men came in within three minutes but it was too late as Mr Kavubu's house was totally consumed in the inferno.

8

The Consequences of Flirtation

Once Upon a Time! There was a beautiful maiden called Oduwa in the land of Ikpoba. She was as tall as a Giraffe, dark in colour as dark chocolate cream and was the dream wife of every young man in the village. Oduwa was born to Osahon and Adesuwa, in a farm settlement area, off the famous Ughoton River where the locals farmed cassava and cocoyam.

Right from birth, Oduwa was said to be special. It was even reported that when her mother was pregnant, a spirit appeared to her and told her that the baby she was carrying was going to be very beautiful. According to customs, this revelation meant that the beautiful girl yet to be born, would elevate the status of the village. This caused a lot of commotion among the locals who were all waiting impatiently, for the birth of the beautiful one.

When the baby was finally born, she was named Oduwa. She had an older sister called Itohan, and both of them were good-looking and caught the attention of men, and even women. Men lined up to win the sisters' hands in love and presented them with gifts such as neck and arm beads, and bangles of all sizes. The traditional bangles represented the pride of the men of Ikpoba, especially in courtship, and the number and sizes of the beads that were presented, personified quality, affluence and the status of the gentleman. Itohan had many of these gifts and almost immediately, began to be lecherous with the aficionados and arrogant towards her family and friends.

As Oduwa and her sister grew up, men continued to struggle to be with them. One of the men was a young and rough looking man called Efe. He was well known for his craftsmanship and like many men, he craved to marry one of the sisters. He had a "crush" on Itohan and longed to take her to the stream and special hideouts. When he started dating her, he discovered that he could not trust her because she told numerous lies and had a promiscuous attitude towards men. In the eyes of the public however, Efe was the lucky man, although Itohan was secretly and constantly meeting other men on the local stream pathway. Efe worried over her unfaithfulness but waited to have strong evidence against her before separating with her.

Meanwhile, Oduwa was disappointed that her older sister was going against traditional values and having relationships outside marriage. Although the tradition required that the older sister got married first, Oduwa was determined to make her life better, even if it meant getting married before her sister. By this time, she was taking an interest in her sister's new boyfriend, Efe.

One evening, Adesuwa and Osahon called their daughters for a special meeting:

"It is time for you to get married", their father said.

Their mother agreed with her husband and reminded the young spinsters that "while it was important for them to get married, it was also significant that the girls understood that tradition conferred special privileges on parents whose daughters were in matrimony". As a result, they urged the girls to get married before it was too late.

The elder daughter, Itohan, spoke first. She told her parents that she was not yet ready to get married. When her parents quizzed her on her relationship with Efe, she answered: "Efe is a man of integrity and candour, and could also be a loving husband, but we are just friends". When Oduwa, who secretly admired Efe, heard this, she took it as a challenge to get together with him.

Without wasting time, Efe and Oduwa got together and spent most of their evenings by the banks of the river. They exchanged gifts such as beads and shells, and even engraved tattoos on special parts of their bodies to mark their love for each other. Their relationship blossomed, and on one of their special nights out, Efe proposed to get married to Oduwa and she accepted without hesitation. Oduwa was overjoyed by the proposal and informed her parents who also received the news with joy and gave them their blessings. The families of the new couple then met and set a date for their traditional marriage rites and elders from the blacksmith's family of Ologbose, led Efe to the Osahons of Ikpoba village in order to perform several marriage rites that included the "rite of wine carrying".

The marriage of Efe and Oduwa, however, brought rivalry and jealousy between the sisters. Itohan was heartbroken by the union and accused her sister of "stealing her man". She claimed that she was the first person to court Efe and so deserved to be married to him. Oduwa, on the other hand, told her sister that she and Efe had developed true love and affection for each other, and were adamant to carry on with the marriage. She also reminded Itohan of the night their parents asked them to settle down in matrimony and she denied that she had any romantic tie with Efe.

The marriage went on as arranged and Oduwa's parents, Adesuwa and Osahon, received their new family-in-laws in a traditional ceremony. The family of Efe presented the new bride with many gifts and even offered her more beads and shells than the rites required. The marriage ceremony lasted for two days and there was abundant food and drinks, and their marriage was spoken about in many villages.

Itohan was left forlorn and although she waited to get married no suitors came her way and so never got married.

9

Cry For a Pair of Shoes

There once lived a single mother who was poor and could not afford a pair of shoe for her daughter. The little girl complained all the time to her mother about going bare feet while many other children had spare shoes and sandals. Despite her numerous complains, her mother was unable to provide her with a pair of shoe or sandals. The little girl then threatened her mother that if she failed to buy her a pair of shoe or sandals, she would go on a hunger strike and die from it.

One day, her mother took her to the local market square where she sold herbs and roots that provided them with their daily meal. As they arrived at the market square and settled in their selling point, the little girl spotted a young boy, about her age who was hopping between crutches that were bigger than him.

Instantly, she felt cold shivers running in her spine and her heart was filled with compassion for him. She wondered to herself: "Oh, how can I be bothering my mother to buy me a pair of shoe when someone else does not have two legs?" "I should be thanking God for giving me two legs and for giving me a mother who loves me unconditionally". "From now onwards, I will not disturb my mother over my lack of shoes", the little girl decided.

The little girl went to school and told her friends about her experience. As she had decided, she never complained about going bare feet.

10

Day I met Mugabe and Tsvangirai

Arm in arm with my Chinese girlfriend, Zheng Luo, we walked straight to the twin door way of the Buckingham Farm Club on the outskirts of Bulawayo City.

"Please, can I see your identity?" A Chinese doorman asked me.

"Definitely", I replied, showing him my DCU identity card.

They allowed Luo and I to go inside but I wondered why the Chinese guards did not ask my girlfriend for her identity too. Then I asked her:

"Babe, why did the guards not ask for your identity?"

"You did not read the invitation card carefully; it is stated that no identification for Chinese girls" Luo replied, smiling.

"And what does that imply?" I asked.

"Perhaps an Afro-Chino intercultural thing", she responded.

We laughed at the incident and just then; the usher came and took us to a special table:

"Sir, what would you like to drink? There is Beer, Wine, Spirit and Champagne." The bar tender offered.

"May I please look at the menu and then come to the counter to take our order?" I said, partially instructing him.

Lee and I perused the list and began searching for the best Zimbabwean beer. As we searched, my eyes caught sight of someone I least expected to see in the club. Then I looked up and realised that many guests were coming from diverse affluent backgrounds. This left me with the feeling that the Buckingham Club was an elite place and I began to settle and enjoy the beauty and extravagance of Chinese culture.

My attention turned back to my table and I teased my girlfriend:

"Come on Babe, you cannot just tell me that this stuff is only meant for Chinese girls".

"I think you have to be more observant the next time you are reading an invitation card", she said in a hushed tone.

Then I looked away and was shocked when I saw the figure of another man I never knew I would ever meet.

"Wow! That's the big man here too. Does it mean he likes this kind of place?" I said, almost shouting.

I watched in amazement as Mugabe went round shaking hands with other guests and sharing jokes.

"I could never have thought that I will ever meet this horrible person in this place, God!" I exhaled.

"Babe, why are you talking like that? Stop speaking that way". Luo advised

We continued arguing over my outburst when I felt a tap on my shoulder. I looked around and saw Mr. Robert Mugabe looking down at us. He said:

"Hello! Young couple, how are you doing?"

"We are doing very well, your Excellency. It is a great Zimbabwean night." We responded at the same time.

"Where are you from, my son, you have a Nigerian accent!" Mr. Mugabe asked.

"Exactly. Your Excellency, I was born and bred in Nigeria but travelled for further studies across the Atlantic", I informed him.

Then, Mr. Mugabe asked Luo if he could step aside with me and exchange a tête-à-tête, and Luo agreed with all pleasure. He took me to a bright angle where there was no noise and told me a very long story about his relationship with the West before he ascended to the seat of power as president of Zimbabwe...

"This is why I look at Morgan with disdain. Many times, I feel like kicking his ass off and even ripping him apart like tomato fruits. I just can't stand that asshole, He is a Brit stooge." Mugabe lamented".

He continued telling me the history of colonial struggle, and talked about his personal involvement many times, and although he tried to make me feel comfortable with him, I still was unable to be. I kept on looking at his clenched fist, which he threatened that he would use on Morgan Tsvangirai and David Cameron or David Miliband if they were ever in a wrestling match.

When Mr. Mugabe spoke about the West's onslaught on Zimbabwe, I could see several signs of stress on him, and my mind wondered whether his veins too could reveal stress signs. If yes, how was he still alive, I doubted.

He talked about the sanctions that have been imposed on his country, ranging from travel, economic to hip hop clothing. "Just look at my outfit tonight; I am in a four piece suit when others are in full hip hop gear and also with bandanas to match. They have even gone as far as frustrating my wife's fashion taste with their ban on almost everything. Next, I am waiting for their ban on the oxygen that I breathe", the President complained to me.

"But why can you not step down after 31years on the "democratic" throne"? I asked

"My son, you will not be able to understand. These people are planning a sinister move when I leave office, and they plan to bring up heavy charges against me", he said.

Then we started discussing on options and safe strategies for him and I sighted someone that looked like Mengistu of Ethiopia in the background. He was walking his ageing legs on the tiles and was arm in arm with an Asian lady. I interrupted Mr. Mugabe and asked him if the man I spotted was Mr. Mengistu and Mugabe said yes! "He is my guest and already feeling at home."

"Have you ever thought of being on a journey with him?" I asked.

"Going to where?" Mugabe asked.

"Perhaps as someone's guest for the rest of your life", I responded.

Mugabe became uncomfortable with my question and led me to the inner rooms of the exquisite club, which was owned by a white Zimbabwean. The guests in the special guest rooms astounded me; I saw Tony Blair sipping a chilled Bulawayo Beer as he explored exit strategies for Mugabe, while Aristide was having a quick nap after consuming a lot of liquor.

Whilst I was trying to recollect the names of some of the old leaders that gathered around Mugabe, I could hear heavy scuffle at the doorway. A fight had broken out between the Chinese Security Team and the tugs of Tsvangirai when they refused to show their identifications.

Hearing about this standoff, Mugabe started to loosen his tie and his suit, threatening to take up a fight with Morgan. The other guests intervened to stop him from engaging in any form of confrontation with Morgan and advised him to take the even as part and parcel of leadership.

It was at this moment that I saw the faces of Mubarak, Ben Ali, Blaise Campaore and Hastings Banda drawing nearer to where Mr. Mugabe was. Then, I heard sounds of gunshots, and my mobile phone rang...

I looked for my phone and found it under my pillow and then I realised that I had been dreaming all night long and had missed twenty-four telephone calls.

11

The story of the Beautiful Maiden

Once Upon a Time! There was a very beautiful Maiden named Mkpurumma who hailed from a humble background but acquired a high standard of living in the days of her ancestors. She came from Mgbidi, the home of Ogbamgba "The Wrestler", who was also nicknamed "The Cat" because of his mastery of the techniques of wrestling. Through his popularity and achievements, the clan of Mgbidi became famous among its neighbours.

Still in the clan of Mgbidi and decades after Ogbamgba "The Wrestler" was dead, another famous child was born. He was named Chinedu, and born into a generation that still enjoyed the fame of their past ancestor and where the women took pride in their men. My Grandfather once told me that the era of Ogbamgba, instilled fear right into many generations and the consequences were many.

Women of neighbouring villages preferred to be married to the men of Mgbidi because they believed that they exhumed more strength and as a result, would protect them better than their own local men. They also believed that men of the clan of Mgbidi were helpful to their families, that they went to the farm and stream with their wives, that they protected their children from slave raiders and were capable of producing beautiful and strong children. With these beliefs, women scrambled to get attention from men of Mgbidi Clan, especially that of Chinedu.

The beautiful maiden, Mkpurumma, was also born into this prestigious clan, alongside many other beautiful maidens. Mkpurumma had an Ebony complexion, she stood as tall as a Gazelle, had a gap between her teeth and stretched her cheeks when she was amused, mannerism that attracted most men to her. In addition to her beautiful and slender looks, Mkpurumma always carried a sense of self-importance around her, and even bore the "Otangele" mark on her firm breasts, which signified substance.

As the saying goes that 'The Beautiful Ones are not Yet Born', the tradition classified girls and gave them marriage grades. In most cases, the grades were rationed and girls of the same age were asked to get married during a special ceremony, and at a certain period. When Mkpurumma and her mates got to the age of marriage, she turned down many

101

requests for marriage that came from young and old men, from wrestlers and princes, because she only had "eyes" for Chinedu, and was waiting to get married to him.

Gradually, all her mates got married and moved to different parts of the village and left her as the only spinster in the village. In the end, Chinedu also got married and to a different maiden that was younger than Mkpurumma. This came as a blow to her and immediately changed her lifestyle. She began idling from one yam barn to cocoyam barn and from one village spot to the next taking delight in gossips while secretly waiting for a better suitor.

Witnessing this for the first time in generations, the elders of the village held a meeting in which they consulted a Diviner to know if the Mermaid Goddess or women of the neighbouring clans had placed a curse on their beautiful daughter. But the Diviner informed them that Mkpurumma was not under the spell of the Mermaid Goddess, neither was she under the curse of other women from neighbouring clans.

Years passed before Mkpurumma realised that she was getting old and losing her beautiful looks. Then, she decided that it was time for her to settle down with a man but was unfortunate because all men rejected her as they had their attentions only on the younger girls, for it is said that "the beautiful ones are not yet born". Frustrated by this humiliation from men, Mkpurumma committed suicide by drowning at the Mgbidi River, which formerly provided a landmark symbol for the clan of Mgbidi.

12

The Story of Onyinye and Her Beloved Son

*A*s previously said, folktales are used to communicate a range of information about African cultures, traditions and values to especially children. Folktales use human and animal characters to communicate values, and though the rights to tell these tales seem to belong to the elders, some parents are passing it onto their own younger children for the sake of posterity.

Some people argue that folktales were only a part of pre-colonial form of knowledge and education in Africa but I disagree. In my opinion, folktales are an important part of modern culture and the art of telling folktales continues to cross over to different generations. It is not a surprise, therefore, that some Africans that have travelled abroad have also brought with them, the culture of telling stories.

Recently, I met a young family with their 13 years-old daughter at a "naming ceremony bash". The young girl approached me and said she had missed out on some of the legendary tales that I write on the newspaper because since her father got a new job, he no longer had time to read the stories to her. I realised just then how much the young generation, especially those born in the West miss out on *rich proverbs and first hand tales from their grandpas and grandmas. It also reminded me of this famous story:*

There was once a man called Okeke who lived in the village of Umueke and got married to three wives. Okeke was well-known for his strength in cultivating lands and filling his barns with yams and other products. As a young man, he was a workaholic; he worked in people's farm lands in exchange for lands, seedlings and other properties and became very rich and famous across many villages and towns. He was so popular that although he had already had three wives, many mothers wanted their daughters to get married to him.

In spite of the number of wives Okeke had, he was not blessed with a male child. (In most parts of Africa, a male child lifts a father's ego among his peers and kin, and preserves his ancestral inheritance, as inheritance was (is) only bequeathed to male offspring. Meanwhile, if a father suddenly died without a male child, his wealth was partitioned among his kin.)

There also lived a maiden, named Onyinye, in this village. Like many young spinsters, she too wanted a piece of Okeke and her mother helped her in the struggle to get married to Okeke. Onyinye made several advances to Okeke and during one farming season, he gave in to her and they had a one night stand. Onyinye got pregnant and later bore Okeke his first boy child who was named Ikenna. With the arrival of his new bundle of joy, Okeke moved Onyinye into his compound but this brought jealousy, rivalry and envy from the other three wives, who soon realised that in order for them to stay married to Okeke, they had to accept the fourth wife who had bore their husband an only son. If they failed to accept her, they knew that Okeke would send them out of his compound.

Okeke loved his only son very much and began to pay more attention to his fourth wife. He constantly bought expensive gifts for his newest wife and his only son, but even this was not enough for Onyinye who was insatiable. She felt threatened every time Okeke occasionally showed love for his other children and wives, and went to a Voodoo Doctor to get advice on what to do. The doctor gave her love portions to add to her husband's meals and assured her that she did not need to worry anymore.

A short time afterwards, two of Okeke's wives bore him two more sons but their arrival failed to excite the husband of four, who once desired to have a battalion of male children in his household. This disturbing change of character in Okeke troubled his first three wives and kin. It was more troubling when the one time strong Okeke began to lose his strength and resolve in deciding over family issues.

Meanwhile, the arrival of Okeke's two other sons heightened Onyinye's fears. She felt that she needed to gain more control of her husband and so sought the help of her mother, Mgbeke. When Okeke failed to show signs of controlling his family, Onyinye and her mother took control of his household and started by dividing his farmlands, and harvest seasons among the three wives. This daring development shocked the other wives, who were already suspecting Onyinye for being responsible for the mayhem going on in their once happy home. Still, Okeke failed to take any action and the first three wives retreated into their separate homes in silence. They also instructed their children to stop going to Onyinye's hut and or playing with her son.

While the other wives watched in silence, Onyinye's mother began to plot the death of her son in-law, without the knowledge of her daughter. She wanted to guarantee that when Okeke died, all of his inheritances would be handed to her daughter and grandson. S0, she visited another Voodoo Doctor and ordered a different type of love portion. The new love portion was designed to be added to his special meal of bitter leaf soup and pounded yam. Her visit to the traditional doctor coincided with the Traditional Nkwo Market Day, a day set aside for fathers to eat with their male offspring and to tell tales that relayed the activities and culture of the ancestors.

When Mgbeke returned from the Voodoo Doctor, she prepared the special bitter leaf Soup and Pounded yam, and added the concoction she had received from the native doctor. She brought the well-garnished meal to her daughter to serve her husband. She, however, warned her daughter that Okeke, must eat the meal alone and oblivious to why her mother gave her this warning, she ignored it. She served the food for her husband and took her only child, Ikenna, to the cassava farm, and instructed the other children to attend to their father after his meal. The children went to join their father but refused to share the meal with their father, even on this special day, as earlier warned by their own mothers.

On the way to the farm, Onyinye realised that she had forgotten her maize seeds at home and sent Ikenna to return home and bring it. When Ikenna arrived home, he saw his father eating while his other brothers sat aside. Without hesitating, he joined his father in his meal before picking up the seeds and then setting back to the farm to join his mother. As he was running, he began to feel very weak, drowsy and wobbly and finally collapsed to the ground.

Meanwhile, Onyinye waited for her son to arrive but to no avail. She began wondering why he had not returned to the farm, hours after she sent him. She left the farm to check what was taking him too long. On her way back home, she found her son lying on the side of the road with white foamy elements coming out on both sides of his mouth and face.

Shocked by this discovery, she carried her son on her left shoulder and began to scream and run for help. When she arrived at the compound, she was still screaming for help and then she noticed that they many people gathered in sorrowful and mourning moods. When she asked what was going on, one of the elders informed her that her husband had died in the same manner as her son, after finishing a bowl of bitter leaf soup and pounded yam. She immediately recollected the warning her mother had given her when she handed her the meal to serve her husband. She realised with disbelief and anger that her mother had just killed her husband and her only son. For, this is how the greedy and egoistic end up. Mgbeke's over ambition cost her, her grandson, her daughter's husband and left her daughter as a widow for life. Now she must face the consequences.

13

I Had a Dream

My father died many years ago, leaving behind a harem of women and many children. I had little knowledge about who my father really was, but I think that his name was spelt like this: "Africanus". I had one male younger sibling, with whom I shared the same mother, and who migrated to a land near the Zambezi River, called Harare.

When I grew up, I became Lord King of Abuja and although I was old enough to retire from active service, I was not ready to leave the position of power and command. Also, I envied my brother, and though he was younger than me, he too was a King in the Southern Land of Harare and was in his 27th year as a ruler. He ruled his land with pride, and brought greatness to his kingdom and in the eyes of the world. He was well respected and any opposition to his throne was met with counter opposition from his supporters, who were said to be countless and compared to the stars in the sky. He was well-liked and loved, and any suggestion that he left the throne was a tabooed subject. So too, I did not want to leave the position of power before my brother.

Even though I envied my brother, I had a palace built on a rock in Abuja and had more riches than him; in fact, I lacked nothing. I commanded a lot of power in my Abuja Kingdom and people came to worship and adore me. Some called me Supreme God and I rewarded them heavily. I gave them access to yam barns, animals, money, property, titles and many other gifts. I even made them to stand out amongst their peers and in their neighbourhoods.

My brother and I had many differences. While I had unattractive and hideous looks, stammered and throttled when I spoke English and my speeches were slurred, my brother was handsome and intelligent. Yet, most people were unaware that I had been very dull in my school days. They even gave me an award as the most successful African Orator, and some people likened me to Emperor Nero of Ancient Rome. While I was happy to be worshipped like the ancient gods and goddesses, I secretly feared that there was going to be a revolution against me.

As King, I discovered the importance of renting crowds and professional clappers. When my advisers first told me that I needed to hire people to attend my functions – the

King's functions if I wanted to succeed, I thought that they had gone blatantly insane. Then, I found out that, while only a few people turned up when I was commissioning a new Brothel for my Ministers, a sea of people turned out during the inauguration of an election campaign. I asked my advisers why this was so. They disclosed to me that during the election campaign, they paid a stipend to each person to be at the launch. My advisers were right after all, and they nick-named the stipend, "the National Cake".

But my reign was not going to last forever without people calling for a change, I lamented to myself one night. Before too long, a few protesters started asking for me to step down from the throne but I could not do this. I was not ready to bear the walk of shame and relinquish my powers while my younger brother was still enjoying the euphoria of leadership in Harare! Also, I could not bear the thoughts of how those stupid coloured people changed power; how could I be witness to my subjects and mad people queuing to drop ballots on who they thought would be suitable for different positions in my kingdom, I wondered? So, I began to bribe my way through attempts to remove me from power.

I decided that I was not going to let them win. I was going to beat them in their own game that they call democracy for *"there are many ways to kill a rat."* Democracy was an absolute demonstration of craziness and I was going to show them how to manipulate the entire process. I began to indulge, together with my ministers, in many more acts of renting crowds and professional clappers who always kept to their own side of the bargain. The rented crowds and professional clappers were always present to fill podiums during our rallies and campaigns. This meant that there was no need for me to go into the villages, jungle inhabited areas or to squalors and shacks to mingle with these people for their desperate votes. I also decided to appoint a poor teacher as the Umpire and my brother's friend as the printer of the ballot papers. I knew that if my brother's best friend were the doorman to the gate of heaven, he would not stop me from gaining entrance, so I had a lot of confidence in him. Also, I was convinced that because I had paid the new Umpire money, he would not repay me badly. In addition, I counted on the cowardice and peaceful nature of my people whom I knew would not put up any resistance against my rule.

Everything happened the way I planned it. Together with my Ministers, Umpire and the Ballot Papers' Printer, I was able to secure my throne again. The coloured people and their democracy, with promises to change the living conditions for the poor could now return to their homes overseas, or face immigration and refugee boom when war breaks out.

Grriiiiiiiiiiii Grriiiiiiiiiiii   Grriiiiiiiiiiii   Grriiiiiiiiiiii...My phone vibrated.

"Who in God's name is this? Who is calling my phone at this sacred hour of the day? I am surely not answering this phone call! By the name of the gods of Asantehene, have I been day dreaming again? I think I need to consult my GP sooner, rather than later, I realised."

14

Oluhara and the Orphan

Oluhara

Once Upon a Time! There was a king in the ancient land of Owere who ruled over nine villages. The king came from a powerful dynasty that was known throughout the rain forest routes for its conquests at wars, but had lost all inheritances passed onto him. Fortunately for him, his ancestral reputation kept the pride of the kingdom intact.

Not too far away from the King's palace, an orphan named, Nwaugo, was living with her uncle. Her uncle was married to Nkechi and they had three daughters and although they were still young, they were older than Nwaugo. Nkechi treated her daughters like princesses but treated Nwaugo like a servant. She assigned Nwaugo to several responsibilities, including washing her cousins' clothes in the village stream, applying mascara and ornaments on them, and preparing food for the household. Nwaugo was also instructed to wake up at the dawn of the cock crow, and before everyone else, to fill water into the clay pots. In addition, she did all farm work on her own and it included, cutting, planting, weeding and harvesting cash crops. Yet, she was not given food; instead, she was made to eat crumbs that fell from the table after the family had eaten.

Nwaugo found it difficult to bear more sufferings and complained to her uncle. She hoped that he would intervene and resolve her difficulties, but he failed to take any corrective actions. With no one else to turn to, Nwaugo cried all nights and called upon her deceased parents to come to her rescue, but nothing happened for a long time. The only thing closed to her was a wooden bed that was made of palm wine branches.

As Nwaugo carried on being a servant, the feast of Oru Owere drew nigh. The festival was celebrated every year at the Central Square and witnessed the exhibitions of products and animals that blessed the lands and fed the people of Owere. The King's Town Crier went out every year, eight market days before the festival, to announce the programme and its modalities; from the sharing of harvested palm fruits, the allocation of virgin forest lands, entertainment from the

113

masquerades at the event square to the selection of the bride.

The selection of the bride was the last and special part of the ceremony. The privileged beautiful maidens of Owere exhibited themselves in front of the Prince (who stood heir to the throne after the passing of the King) with the hope of "catching" his attention for a hand in marriage. This parade went on every year until the Prince found a wife – the next Princess and subsequent Queen of the Land and so maidens took it very seriously.

They braided new hairstyles, did body painting on strategic parts of their bodies, ordered for newer clothes, newer beads for their necks, hair, wrists and waists, and took every year as a stronger competition. If and when the Prince finally chose a wife, women matched to the centre to pray over the final choice of the Prince. The new mother-in-law was then presented with barns full of yam and cocoyam, many hectares of farmland and automatically gained respect from other women from that moment onwards because she bore the wife of the prince.

When the day of the festival came, Nwaugo's three cousins were among other locals who put on their best garments and went to the village square. Before setting out to the square, Nkechi instructed Nwaugo to make her daughters look their personal best and to stay at home after that. Once they left, Nwaugo burst into tears and then became unable to bear the echoes of the festival coming from the village square. She did what most little girls would do and left the house. She too secretly wished to be married to the Prince. (She thought about the saying: "If wishes were horses, beggars would ride on them" and knew it was an illusion to think of ever getting married to a Prince.)

She put her thoughts aside and put on her rags and went out for sightseeing. A parcel at the corner of the muddy hut caught her attention and she went to pick it. When she opened it, she found that the parcel contained new weaved clothes, beads, beauty body paints and ornaments of the highest quality that would distinguish any girl from other maidens. She contemplated why the parcel was there and made a decision.

She changed into the outfit and ran down the path that led to the community square, but as she approached the centre, she was suddenly overtaken by fright. She thought about what would happen to her if Nkechi and her daughters saw her at the square and decided to stay by the edge of the path and watch from the distance.

As Nwaugo was fixing herself in the hideout, the prince was making his entrance into the village square, through the same short route that she had used. His entourage drove pass and the Prince spotted a girl hiding and he wondered what she was doing there. He got taken in by the beauty of the girl and ordered his driver to stop, and he alighted from his royal wagon. He came up to the girl and asked her why she was staying there and not at the square. When the Prince noticed that the maiden was too shaken to speak, he told her to come to the square and model with the other maidens. He then left to join the rest of the convoy and they went to the square.

When the last stage of the ceremony was announced, all the maidens came out, clothed in their most cherished regalia and ready to impress the Prince. They started modelling and the last person to show up was Nwaugo who had summed up the courage to heed to the Prince's advice. She walked past and heard the crowd's sighs of embarrassment, rejection and even horror, but she managed to complete her parade. The crowd then waited in tranquillity, and at that moment, just that one moment in the silence of the festivity, one could hear the sound of a pin drop, as everyone waited; some in anticipation, for what could be a remarkable day in a maiden's life.

When the Prince stood up from his chair to make his choice and take his bride home, there was even more silence. He walked majestically from one maiden to the other and from the last to the first and then to the last and finally picked the maiden who was hidden on the bush path. The entire crowd went still for some time, horrified by the choice he had made, for it was known that she was a pauper and not good enough to be with other maidens, even more so, to stand as wife of the Prince, their new Princess and potentially their new Queen.

Unfortunately, tradition had set its rules even before the Prince was born. The Prince had the final say on whom he desired to be his bride and this was not reversible, only because he had chosen a poor servant who was also an orphan. The other maidens felt that they were the rightful choice and were jealous and enraged most especially, Nwaugo's cousins and their mother, who felt that Nwaugo had wrongfully taken their place. They wondered how a dejected orphan could attract the eyes of the Prince of Owere, but it was too late now as the Prince had chosen his bride and she was now a Princess and future Queen of the land of Owere. Nkechi and her daughters walked home in shame and with regrets over the bad manner in which they treated their cousin and kin.

15

The Pharisee

From the Holy Scripture, many things were said about the Pharisee. Like then, there are similar stories in today's world: their peacock-like characteristic can be found in many top people, such as celebrities, top actors and actresses, rock and hip hop stars, business magnets, religious leaders, top professionals and world acclaimed philanthropists. Among them are also Politicians who are the greatest peacocks and who, most often, feel that they are the beginning and end of a law. They smile at the sweat of poor

hardworking people, shed tears like crocodiles in their presence but wink behind their backs. Before I go on, I should tell you this story:

There once were two men in a predominant Christian community who regularly went to church to pray. One owned a chain of businesses in the town and was extremely wealthy and decided to run in the upcoming elections. A reliable source claimed that his interest in politics was to protect his abundant businesses and not the local community, but like the adage says that "the heart is like a hand bag, only the owner knows what is inside", it was never known why he ventured into politics. However his intentions, he also decided to seek the intervention of the supernatural being through supplication.

The second man was a wretched married man and father of four children. He was an unskilled labourer and exploited by many people because he badly needed to provide a meal for his family; as a result, his several employers paid him lower than other workers. He was so miserable that he considered it a luxury when he was able to provide two meals per day for his family.

One day when the church was empty and the tabernacle was opened for people to submit their needs in prayers, the poorer man came in first. He went straight to the front of the altar and knelt on the floor and began to cry and talk in a loud voice to an invisible God. He told God that he was not going to go home and would stay at the foot of the altar until his prayers were answered or until he had a miracle.

While he remained at the foot of the altar weeping and praying, the rich man turned politician came into church. Clad in a costly robe and smelling of an affluent and beautiful fragrance, he came to pray for his success at the elections and other interests. He went directly to the front pew and sat on the seat that was permanently reserved for him, whether he came to mass or not. As he started praying, the cry of the man at the foot of the altar became too loud for him to concentrate on his prayers. Feeling that the man's cry was acting as a hindrance to his relationship with God, he went up to the poor and wailing man on the floor.

He tapped at his shoulder and said to him: "How much do you really need so that you could leave the church as your weeping is distracting my prayers?"

"Just a little that can fetch bread for my starving family", the weeping man replied.

The politician dipped his hand into his pocket and came out with a bundle of money and gave it to the man. The weeping man wiped his tears and was "in the seventh heaven" over the amount of money the man dished out to him. The money was more than he had ever earned and he ran home in jubilation to share the wonders of God's miracle with his family. Meanwhile, the Politician continued to battle his problems in prayers, totally unaware of the impact of his kind gesture to the crying man.

16

The Midnight Mad Man

There was once a mentally disturbed man called Timothy, who lived in the market square. He lived in a ramshackle home that was besides the main shrine of the divine being of the community, which the locals worshipped before the advent of Christianity. Although Timothy suffered from mental illness, he spoke within clear and wise thoughts. He also spoke like a seer and prophet, and often told people that his place of residence gave him access to see beyond the night. When he spoke however, no one paid any attention to his thoughts because of his mental deficiency.

On one midnight when heavy rainfall descended on the town and its environs, Timothy saw, through holes of his squalor, a man committing a gruesome crime. He recognised the man as one of the prominent leaders in the church council who always sat next to the Pastor during church worship and services. Timothy looked closely and witnessed the Church Leader, together with the help of some thugs strangling his half-brother. His first instinct was to go out to help but was too frightened to move to the bloody scene. When the beaten man slung to the floor, the assassins fled the scene. Timothy then rushed to the man but realised that the victim was already death.

On the evening of the burial for the murdered man, Timothy joined many of the mourners for the requiem mass. When he entered the church, he saw the Church Leader who had led thugs to kill his brother seated in the front pew and sandwiched among friends. He had tears rolling down his cheeks at the sight of his half-brother's coffin.

Timothy watched in anger and horror at the man's hypocrisy and leaped towards him but was grabbed by the Church Warders and bundled out of the church. As they led him outside, he began kicking his feet in the air and shouting that the Church Leader was the murderer. Timothy said that he saw the church leader murdering his half-brother, with the help of his friends. He added that the murderer should be deposed from his position in Church and taken to court to face murder charges, but no one that heard him in the church believed him. They simply considered his words as those of a mad man, which he was, and no one trusted him. Unfortunately, only the dead can truthfully say who their killers are.

17

The Wicked Stepmother

Once Upon a Time! There lived a rich man in the village of Mbaise. The village was situated in the hinterland and located off the path of the coast of the Niger. The rich man was called Anyanwu, meaning "The Sun", as advised by Amuzi, the voodoo priest. When Anyanwu was born, his parents consulted Amuzi to know what his future would be. The voodoo priest predicted that the tot would be a man of great wealth and that his riches would be as imposing as the moon. Thus, the baby was named Anyanwu, "The Sun".

As predicted by the voodoo priest, Anyanwu's wealth was endless, so too, was his kindness towards people in need.

He opened the doors of his house to those in need of food and water, and his benevolence was never-ending. People talked about his philanthropic characteristics, so much so that the elders of the community decided to confer a title on him. They choose the title of Ezeji, meaning "King of Yams" and the new status gave him an even bigger edge over all sons and daughters of Mbaise.

Anyanwu had a son, called Aboh, with his wife who sadly died when Aboh was just ten years old. Anyanwu then remarried one of his wife's maids, who already was taking care of his only son. He felt that marrying the caretaker of his son would also mean giving his son another mother. He got married to the maid called Nwanyi Ojoo, who bore him one son and two daughters. Nwanji, however, changed and became a nagging woman, to everyone around her, including her former employer who was now her husband, her step son and former co-workers.

Although she was blessed with three children and enough wealth, Nwanyi wanted, Aboh, who was the right heir to his father, death. She prayed that he should die so that all his father's inheritances would be passed over to Nwanne, her own biological son. She maltreated Aboh and made him to do all the house chores. Often, she left Aboh without food and starving, and at other times, she sent him to eat second best meals with other maids, as a sign of humiliation. She even turned her children against their step brother and two of them stopped playing with him. She also handed them a list of Do's and Dont's regarding Aboh.

Ezinne was one of Nwanyi's daughters and had a lot of compassion for Aboh. She stayed with him when he was lonely, cried with him when he cried, and assisted him with household chores that her mother gave him. One day, Ezinne prepared a meal of roasted yams for Aboh who was starving, but her mother beat her so badly that she ended up with torn lips.

Whilst this went on, Ezeji was watching, totally powerless, and incapable of stopping his own son from becoming a servant. Constantly, he thought of divorcing Nwanyi or sending her out of his house but the thoughts of what people would make of him always stopped him.

On one Eke market day when most people were in the Village Square doing trade by barter, she cooked a meal of Egusi soup and grinded cassava (fufu) and garnished it attractively for Aboh. She instructed Aboh that he was not to eat the special food unless he finished his chores. She then took her three children and set off to the cocoyam farm to join her husband.

Feeling excited that his step-mother appreciated his hard work, Aboh decided to work even harder. In the farm, his three siblings sat by the barn and roasted cocoyam while their parents worked. Suddenly, Nwanne started to vomit blood and food particles and his parents rushed to his side. They harvested traditional herbs to stop the sickness and revive him, but this proved abortive and they took him back home. Nwanne died on the way back but before he died, he accused Aboh of poisoning his food.

Holding his son in his hands, Ezeji ran to the compound to check what was left of his other son. People who gathered at the market square saw him running and followed him to his compound to find out what was wrong. When he arrived at the compound, Aboh was still doing his house chores before eating his own share of the food. Ezeji rushed towards his only surviving son and grabbed him and hugged him and cried out loud: "Thank the gods, thank the gods." Unknown to them, Nwanyi had poisoned food that was to be given to Aboh but gave it to her own son instead - food that finally killed her beloved son.

Ezeji summoned the elders and villagers to his compound and recounted the ordeal he had suffered in the hands of his second wife, Nwanyi Ojoo. When the elders and the villagers heard this heart wrenching story, they ruled that Nwanyi would be immediately driven away from the village. They gave her the traditional broom and sent her into the evil forest that contained spirits and wild animals.

Ezeji decided that he would no longer marry again and stayed with his three children happily after. For the time being, the punishment meted out to Nwanyi served as a lesson to all step-mothers and wicked women in the village.

18

The Rainmaker and The Wedding

I was already an adult when I arrived in Europe, but I could not help but be baffle by the climate. Although climatic conditions are the works of nature and the creator, I wondered how people were walking around, and those that walked before them, how they survived or relaxed in freezing temperatures. I was even more surprised that most of the Europeans I met dreaded the chilling winter and or, blazing summer, just like most of us from warmer zones, and I reflected on the reasons bees retreat to beehives for summer activities, why holidays, ceremonies and functions abound in the summer and why meteorological science emerged.

This branch of natural science continues to develop. It has upgraded rapidly in contemporary times but also has some shortcomings because the information is only limited to certain targeted areas, time and depth of damage or occurrences. On the other hand, in some parts of Africa, it is common knowledge that people still possess powers to make or mar rain from falling. Some of our elders told us stories about rainmakers and of the few, but powerful rainmakers who received accolades from possessing this rare quality. And when I was fourteen years old, I witnessed, for the first time, a classical demonstration of the art of stopping a downpour of rain.

*   *   *

I heard noises coming from the "Parlour" and I went in to check. I saw some elders cleaning kola nuts and getting ready to pour libations. They were also hailing a young man for having done a great job for the Okonkwo's family a few weeks ago. On the side, I saw my father, Ukachukwu Okoro Senior, and a young man talking over a keg of fresh wine, which was just tapped from the palm kernel tree.

I called my father to the side and asked him who the youngest of the men was. He told me that his name was Ikemefula and that he was about twenty years old and was the youngest rainmaker in and around the Old Owerri villages. My father also told me that Ikemefula hailed from a lineage of rainmakers and that his great-great-grandfather was noted for wining a dispute over an ancestral forest, which almost stopped the celebration of the New Yam Festival.

Ikemefula! One of the elders saluted, "you are a true lion in this town".

"You are the true son of your father", the other elder joined in.

"Ukachukwu Okoro," the first elder called out to my father: "this young man, pointing to Ikemefula, is as strong as his grandfather and as the fathers before him. He held the cloud at Okonkwo's place despite the threat of enemies. He is the pride of our town".

128

When my father heard these tributes, he asked if Ikemefula would be willing to hold back the rain on the day of my aunt's wedding rites that were scheduled during the Christmas holiday. My aunt was my father's younger sister and best friend, and my dad wanted to give her a memorable marriage gift – one that had no rainfall to damper her big day. Ikemefula said he would be honoured to do the job for my dad and they both set terms on which they were going to work, including the length of time Ikemefula was going to hold the rain from falling.

On the morning of my aunt's wedding day, there was a downpour of rain and it seemed as if it would not stop, and the bride-to-be began to worry and weep. She wept as though she had lost someone, but her weeping soon turned to disbelief when Ikemefula strolled in from the gate. He walked in a serene manner and without any wetness on him or his clothes, although "the heavens had opened" and there was a sea of water pouring from the sky.

He went to the backyard, towards the end of the wall and arranged a fire from a log of wood. Still in the downpour, I watched as Ikemefula brought out green leaves, alligator pepper, white chalk and broken tree branches and started to give instructions to the rain.

He poured libation on the earth and showered encomiums to his dead father and ancestors, and asked them to arise and do what their family was known for. Ikemefula continued this battle with the rain for about twenty minutes before a strong lightening tore through the cloud and rain, sending a thunderous noise and instantly cutting off the downpour in the village where my aunt's wedding was taking place.

It was simply a miracle and one that was witnessed by a newer generation. For the duration of the wedding rites, there was not a drop of rainfall in the village, but confirmed reports in nearby villages said the downpour-seizure-marvel did not extend to them; on the contrary, it continued for two more days.

In the end, my aunt's wish came true. She had a successful wedding in which Ikemula also "held the rain" from falling. When the ceremonies ended and almost everybody had left, Ikemefula said he had accomplished his mission and left for his house. As soon as he left, the downpour started all over again.

My aunt's wedding and the miracle of the dry weather became "the next big thing" across many villages.

19

The Fasting Monks

At the start of the 20th century, a group of Monks lived in a monastery that was located off the coast of Africa. The monks devoted time to pray to God to save the world from imminent destructions. They also lived by principles that included seclusion and abstinence from earthly things. These characteristics exhibited by the monks inspired people to ask them to mediate in their requests with the Almighty. People came with different kinds of problems, which ranged from family feuds, poor harvest seasons, to socio-cultural crisis.

The Monks set up different sub groups and divided the dedicated requests and prayer points among the groups, in order to facilitate the requests of the people. At this time, the whole village was confronted by an epidemic that threatened to engulf all people, and the monks believed that the solution was to fast and pray. Then, they decided to pray and fast for 48 hours, with the hope that God would give them the best result and eradicate the epidemic.

On the first day of their fasting period, some monks from a sister-monastery came to visit the Leader of the Monks. Seeing that his guests were so worn out and hungry, he went to prepare food and warm water for them. As he arranged the fire, the chimney sent smoke and flames to the sky, and this surprised the other Monks who were not allowed these distractions for 48hours.

The rest of the Monks went to find out why their Superior was desecrating their holy task and sabotaging their mission. As they opened the door to his office, they saw the leader putting a junk of the guest food into his mouth.

"What!" They all exclaimed.

"Why are you eating when we are meant to be fasting", they asked him.

The Superior explained to them that the tradition required him to be a good host, which included tasting food before guests could eat. When he finished explaining to the other Monks, he concluded with this Hymn: *"Whatsoever you do to the least of my brothers, that you do unto me. When I was homeless, you gave me a home, When I was hungry you gave me to eat, now enter into the home of my father."*

"God will unquestionably understand that hospitality is as good as other major factors of godliness", he said.

20

WHY THE VULTURE HAS NO FRIEND

Once upon a time in the land of animals and birds, there was peace and love between all. Birds and animals of all kinds lived together in harmony. All shared apartments tunneled in caves as birds even weaved nests in human caves. The earth was filled with brotherhood as much as green food was plenty. As the population of the earth grew, it was agreed that their must be leadership and authority vested in either an animal or bird. However, it was decided that it must rotate between them. The birds, after much discussion, conceded the first shot at leadership to the animals. They told the animals to decide among themselves and present the first Emperor of the earth as agreed.

As such, all animals presented a man and the earth came under his authority unanimously. The birds tallied along with the hope of succeeding man after his death. Unfortunately for the birds, there was a conspiracy between humans and other animals. They planned to short-change the birds and rotate it between them instead.

It happened that during the reign of the humans, there was drought on earth as no rain dropped from the sky for a couple of years. This brought tough times on earth as the human leadership demanded hard work and commitment from all in communal effort to grow drought friendly crops. As this period demanded serious manual labour from all, it was evident that the vulture was lazy and cunning. They would laze around only to eat more to annoy other birds and animals. The human leadership did not take this kindly as they felt cheated by a little creature without bigger brains.

This trend continued until life came back like it used to be but sooner rather than later, the Emperor died. The death threw the throne open but it was previously agreed that the next occupant shall be one of the birds. Though grudgingly, humans and their counterparts asked the birds to nominate among them. After tough deliberations and arguments, the birds came up with the choice of the vulture but it perturbed all how it came to happen.

The humans were the first to object to the choice, arguing about the vulture's laziness in the case of tough times. Other animals joined the humans in backing off from recognizing the bird's choice and soon, there was a crisis of leadership. The birds agreed to back the vulture due to certain strange qualities it possessed that frightened the animals, of which some included patience and cunningness. However, their support became shaky as the whole issue threatened earthly harmony, making them begin to withdraw their support for the vulture.

Meanwhile, chaos started to set in when other animals sought the backing of humans to reign as they had agreed but the latter backed off, instead manoeuvering to continue leading with the pretence of holding forth until calm was restored. However, the birds regrouped and nominated another to replace the vulture but the victim could not take it. On the other hand, crisis of confidence brewed between the animals over the craftiness of humans.

Finally, war seemed imminent and the vulture took his offspring off with a parting warning to other birds to watch out for the worst of humans and their fellow animals. For all animals, he promised to stage a come-back for revenge at the right time. A war later broke out on earth when the vulture and its lineage were out. As a form of payback, they always hovered and patiently perched mocking a dying animal or bird to give up fast so they could eat it as a way of pay-back. Since that earthly war, they do not mix with other birds or animals because of lack of trust.

Part Three: Proverbs
(Bonus Section)

1

Classical African Proverbs

Culture could be summarised as people's way of life, but scholars have proffered different explanations and depending on their schools of thought.

Culture is defined by *Oxford English Dictionary for students (2006)* as the art, custom, ideas, and social behaviour of a nation, people, or group.

A recent survey on peoples' cultural understandings revealed that although ways of life vary among different cultures and people, all human beings are the same. It was also noted that the identity of mankind makes it easy for people to assimilate other cultures. For example: Although foods differ from people to people, they perform the same function in every digestive system.

Culture, as a nation's way of life has components that make it distinctive and particular. Africa, for example, is unique to Africans because of their grasp on culture despite some dissenting views across the Atlantic. Although African studies are quite limited in European citadels of wisdom, African cultures are now finding their ways into the hearts of a handful of Europeans that thirst for information and knowledge beyond their frontiers. If you believe that culture is knowledge, you can also concur that wisdom, which is knowledge in this context, can be divided into two forms: academic and natural.

Until the advent of colonisation, Africans practised the natural way of knowledge, which has resisted onslaught and annihilation. This system of knowledge includes the art of storytelling, exploiting the gift of the environment and invoking the supernatural.

The art of storytelling has many aspects, but the remarkable aspects are classical proverbs and idioms that buttress points of speech. Our elders say that "proverbs and idioms are the palm oil our people use in eating words."

It is therefore, my pleasure to share with you, especially the young ones, some classical proverbs, idioms and their close meanings.

Proverb / Idioms	Meaning
"The chameleon says he will never abandon the dignified walking ways of his father just because the bush is burning."	It means that a principled one never flip-flops from his ideals no matter the circumstance.
"A child carried at the back does not know how far the journey is."	A lazy person never feels the pains of suffering.
"He, who the gods have blessed, let him spread it around."	It pays to be benevolent
"It is a mark of respect to the fire that the pot stays on it without complaint and it is also a mark of regard that the fire does not set the pot ablaze but only cooks its contents."	Respect is reciprocal
"The head that sinks is not always as big as the earth."	No human being is infallible.
"When a child washes his hands clean, he dines with elders."	The association of progressives has no age barrier.
"When a child chooses to be a prodigal son, he becomes one."	She, who fails to plan, plans to fail.
"The toad does not scamper in vain during the noon."	Danger has no specific time frame.
"It is not how long a snake is that makes it dangerous, it is the venom that it carries that makes it deadly."	Reputation and integrity is built through consistent steadfastness.
"A child that grows teeth is no longer a toddler."	The measurement of an achiever is his achievements.

"A wise man takes his time to like a hot soup."	A star is a celebrity
"If the eyes shed tears, it affects other parts of the head."	Planning breeds success.
"The woman who fetches ant infested firewood calls for a lizard's party."	A national calamity concerns all.
"The head that upsets the beehive let him bear the pain of the bee hive."	He, who likes trouble, gets into danger.
"The back that falls to the ground in a contest shall be rubbed with the sand."	The criminal gets punishment.
	Absolute honesty cannot be diluted.

EXERCISE SECTION

Proverb	Meaning
"The eyes eat before the mouth"	
"A man who sleeps with the widow is not afraid because he knows where the husband is"	
"You know the kind of shit from the smell of the fart"	
"The eagle has not been caught and it is said that women do not eat it"	
"When a finger is dipped in oil, it touches others"	
Stubborn flies ends up with corpse in the grave"	
"As long as the penis continues to live, it must eat the beaded meat"	
"Licking hot soup requires slow and patience"	
"Wherever a child is crying for hunger, the relative must be around"	
"An elder cannot watch a goat give birth in a stead "	
"Whatever taste so sweet, kills too"	

"The god that made yam grow for a poor man shall provide digger to harvest it"	
" The owner of the barn has the yam as well as the knife"	
"The rain that soaked the eagle just washed it up"	
"Have no fear of perfection, you will never reach it"	

AUTHOR'S NOTES:

The usage of words as seen above describes the core and interactive ethics of the African culture. It is important that young African know their roots and culture. It is the African's way of life and cannot be erased.

Harmattan is a season in Nigeria and some parts of Africa that brings in cold and harsh weather conditions from the Atlantic.

This story tells you to avoid swanking because no one knows what tomorrow will bring.

We all learn life from our elders and parents throughout our formative years and beyond. Although this tale is unwritten, the likes of these stories have helped me and other Africans to "weather the storms of life".

After an historic leadership tussle, the Antelope won the elections and the reign of the Elephant shamefully came to an end in what has now been put by Elders from my hometown as: 'A kindred can finish the meal cooked by one person but the latter cannot finish the meal prepared by the former'.

This story teaches us to always listen to good advice and watch for telling signs for "there cannot be any smoke without fire." Ikemefula failed to listen to advice and got married to his dead wife's maid who was rumoured to be malicious. It was the same rumoured woman who finally sent him to the grave.

Visit St Peters Church, Phibsboro in Dublin during the period of "The New Yam Festival" to witness and to benefit the essence of harvest thanksgiving. Above everything, it will showcase the spirit of togetherness and the celebration of faith in the Supreme Being. A visit to such a function is a practical lesson.

This story should serve as a lesson to everyone that you must never neglect, reject, bully or harass anyone in life
.Dependence on a certain lifestyle has to give way to newer horizons and heeding to advice from experts will always most certainly pay out than be bad. Most importantly, always listen to the cry of children for it is a ground-breaking chance to make positive changes.

Addiction to any type of life is as dangerous as the act itself and should be averted. I strongly believe that most Africans still practise this lifestyle and it is time they look into its downsides and make positive changes, for no child is born dull. Children are a gift and they are born with different gifts and or talents

An African adage says: "With knowledge, there is more wisdom to academic brilliance than breaking of the classroom chalk." This means that the family is always the first important classroom for a child regardless of western education. More so, the Mother is the first partner in teaching a child how to talk. Therefore, I pledge that mothers should be the ace in a child's behavioural attitude and parents must bear the responsibility of bringing up their children responsively.

This story should serve as a lesson to people who believe in impressing other people by using unconventional language or language that is difficult to understand. Avoid big blown grammar.

This story serves as a good lesson for people who are not committed in relationships.

For it is said that: "The beauty of a woman is like a Rose Flower; it shines in the morning and quickly fades in the evening".

There is always retribution for the injustice that people do to others and as the saying go: *"The Evil that men do live after them"* in most cases it is: *"the evil that men do live with them."*

One word, they say, is enough for the wise

The process of stopping the rain from falling was like a miracle to me, but people attribute this special talent to good genes. And I am thinking that this kind of talent would be very good for Ireland. For the purpose of information, I heard that Ikemefula is still alive and continuing with holding and bringing the rain at different seasons.

Other Books by Ukachukwu Okorie include:

1. In the Jungle of Europe
2. Across the Liffey River
3. Nigeria Weeps
4. Whither Ndigbo
5. The Giant's Political Crossroad